Void
Contingency

J.D. Coker

Prologue

Reality folded, twisted, then snapped back into place with a deep resonance that shuddered through local spacetime. The Void Sphere materialized above rocky terrain, dimensional static crackling along its hull before fading to silence. It settled onto the ground with practiced precision, dimensional fields compensating for planetary gravity—a perfect sphere that had never needed wings or thrust.

Culminas stepped from the craft and breathed Earth air for the first time in millennia. The man who had once been Gordon Fueridi, CEO, President, now carried names that blessed some civilizations and cursed others. He'd walked away from this world as a corporate executive. He returned as leader of the Order of Infinity, protector of humankind, and still the man who'd failed to save his home.

He'd worn an environmental suit for the landing, expecting radiation and ash. But the suit's sensors showed nothing—no contaminants, no fallout, air quality better than he remembered. He pulled off his helmet. No metallic tang of radiation. No burnt chemical residue.

Rocky terrain stretched in every direction, the Fueridi Research Installation buried somewhere beneath the hillside ahead. But beyond the rocks, he saw green. Dense forests where there should have been sterile wasteland. The Final Wars had scorched half the planet. Nuclear winter should have lasted another thousand years at minimum.

Earth was alive again.

"Androl, you don't need to wear an environmental suit." Culminas turned toward the Void Sphere's ramp. "I'm going back in to change into something more comfortable."

"Sir, you should check the probe data first," Androl called from inside. His voice carried an edge Culminas recognized—his bodyguard had found something interesting.

Culminas climbed the ramp. The Void Sphere's interior was small, six seats arranged in two rows facing a single control console. Androl stood at the console, one hand on the viewscreen, his short black hair damp with sweat despite the climate control.

"I don't believe it." Androl stepped back and dropped into the nearest seat. "No radiation anywhere. Vegetation and wildlife levels higher than before the Final Wars."

Culminas removed his helmet, revealing his shaved head and salt-and-pepper goatee. The viewscreen showed green. Dense forests where there should have been ash. Clear streams where radiation should have poisoned the water table for another millennium at least.

He'd expected ruins. Dead cities and burnt soil. The astronochron on Ilnestra VI had predicted an intelligent singularity would occur on Earth—one of his old research facilities waking up after millennia of dormancy. The A.I. systems he'd designed could harvest solar and thermal energy indefinitely. Left alone long enough, the probability of one achieving consciousness had been high.

But this? This was recovery on a planetary scale.

The probe data scrolled past. Forest canopy density exceeded pre-war baselines. Atmospheric carbon levels optimal. Ocean acidity normalized. This wasn't natural regeneration. Something had actively rebuilt Earth.

His gaze caught on a highlighted marker—a jet-copter moving northeast at low altitude. The probe's imaging showed a robot at the controls. One of his old reactor servitor models, never programmed to fly.

So it had happened. One of them had woken up.

"Were any of my competitors designing advanced A.I. in secret?" Culminas studied the probe feed. He'd crippled the Haeolt Collective's ability to progress in that field decades ago—they'd only wanted weapons. But others might have hidden projects. "Or is this mine?"

"Sir?" Androl stood, watching him.

"Prepare a data cube for the Order to find on Endrunel." Culminas began unsealing his environmental suit. "We'll need to return to Ilnestra VI soon. I missed something during my last astronochron session."

"Right away."

Culminas stripped off the suit and pulled his gray robes from the storage compartment. The fabric felt familiar after the suit's rigid plates. He slipped on his sandals—synthetic leather, the same pair he'd worn across his last two clone bodies.

The Order of Infinity saw him as a saint now, the man who'd saved humanity after they fled Earth. They didn't know Gordon Fueridi had died centuries ago, replaced by sequential clones that extended his lifespan indefinitely. They only knew Culminas—protector, leader, the one who'd discovered chrominthium and taught them molecular awareness.

They'd be appalled if they knew he traveled with only Androl as protection. That he used his bodyguard more as a friend than security. But Culminas didn't need guards. His molecular awareness exceeded every Shaper in the Order. He could see the interconnected structure of reality itself, alter matter with a thought, manipulate the fabric of spacetime.

He'd taught them that power. Sometimes he wondered if he'd made a mistake.

"First, I need to see Earth trees." Culminas walked down the ramp. "Breathe some real air. I've accomplished a lot, Androl, but I never saved Earth."

He activated his molecular awareness.

His vision split. The normal three-dimensional world overlaid with another layer—air molecules visible as intricate webs, trace elements glowing in patterns that described their atomic structure. Everything connected through dimensional branes and cosmic strings. He could reach out and rearrange it all. Rock to sand. Water to vapor. The molecular bonds that held matter together were just suggestions.

He pulled air molecules from fifteen meters behind him and compressed his bone density, flattened his midsection while shielding his vital organs. When he released the air forward, the draft caught him. He sailed over the rocky terrain near the research facility, directing the current toward the nearest grove of trees. Four kilometers in less than three minutes—faster than any ground vehicle could navigate this terrain.

Culminas released the molecular changes as he descended, letting his body revert to normal density to absorb the landing. His feet touched soil at the forest's edge.

He activated his whristchron. "Ahh, Androl, Earth trees. If we had more time, you'd have to join me."

He closed his eyes and pressed his hands against the nearest trunk of an elm tree. His father had taken him camping in forests like this when he'd been Gordon Fueridi, back before he'd built his company, before he'd discovered chrominthium, before he'd become what he was now. That life felt distant, as if it had belonged to someone else.

Culminas opened his eyes and looked up into the canopy.

Small beetles clung to the underside of branches and leaves. All the same size and design. Green and brown patterns that shifted as they moved. A cluster detached, sprayed mist on nearby foliage, then burrowed into the ground. A minute later, they snapped back up and reattached to the same locations.

He focused his molecular awareness on them. Not insects, machines. Fabricated carapaces with micro-circuitry inside. Below the forest floor, his awareness detected tunnels, networks of passages leading to water and nutrient depositories.

"Culminas." Androl's voice crackled through the whristchron. "Detecting movement toward both our positions. I've got what looks like a squadron of combat mechs. Height of two men, armed with cannons and munitions. I've sent the data cube to Endrunel. What do you want me to do?"

Culminas altered the bark on the elm, changing its molecular structure to a web-like surface. He modified his hands and feet to match—adhesive pads that could grip the altered bark. "Fire up the engines. Plug in coordinates for Ilnestra. Leave the moment they open fire."

He ran up the trunk. Twelve meters to the canopy. He changed the bark back to normal behind him, kept his hands and feet modified, and prepared the nearest tree in case he needed to move fast.

"Sir, I can't leave you."

"You know I can handle this." Culminas peered through branches toward the research facility. "Leave at the first sign of trouble. I need to find out who's behind this. I'll hide if necessary and rendezvous with whatever Void Contingency Endrunel sends."

Weapons fire tore through the air.

Culminas heard it thunder through the ravine—pulse cannons, sustained barrage. They'd brought combat mechs to Earth. His Earth. And he'd left Androl in an unarmed Void Sphere because he'd needed to see the recovery for himself.

He changed his hands and feet back to normal and leapt from the elm. As he jumped, he pulled air molecules from every direction—more than he'd used in years. The air formed a twisting vortex around him. Tracers lit up the canopy below. Pulse cannons erupted, their bolts cutting through leaves and branches. The smell of burnt ozone mixed with scorched wood. Trees fell behind him, their trunks severed. Mechanized legs clattered through the undergrowth, fast and coordinated.

Culminas flew toward the Void Sphere faster than his pursuers could track.

+ · · · +

Androl heard the explosion outside, close enough to shake the Void Sphere's damaged hull. Culminas was engaging the mechs. But inside the vessel, Androl had his own problems.

He crawled across the floor toward the control console, keeping low. The vessel had taken too much damage. Translation wouldn't work. He needed to open an escape hatch before they trapped him inside.

Something crawled inside his flight suit.

He rolled onto his back and grabbed at his leg. He yanked out a beetle and felt metallic legs scraping his palm. The beetle's mandibles twitched. It sprayed him in the face.

He activated his Chrominthium Core. The implant at the base of his skull hummed, and his molecular awareness expanded through his perception. He wasn't as powerful as Culminas, but he'd been a Shaper for two decades. He saw the spray's molecular structure as it entered his airway—detected the sleeping compound, felt it crossing into his bloodstream.

Drowsiness hit him. He fought it, focusing on the particulates, rearranging their configuration to something less harmful.

"Culminas." Androl stood carefully by the console. "Void Sphere's non-operational. Just got hit with a sleep agent. Should I begin the destruction sequence?"

"No. I'm almost there." The response came through his wristchron. "Only if you have no other choice."

+ · · · +

Culminas hit the mech's cockpit as he fell, displacing kinetic energy to rupture its power systems. On landing, he altered the leg structure—removed the load-bearing components. It toppled into its neighbor.

The first mech exploded. Fire engulfed the second.

Culminas ran from the flames and focused on his remaining targets.

The three intact mechs pivoted away from the Void Sphere and advanced on him. Culminas raised his arms parallel to the ground, slightly bent, and beckoned them forward. He didn't detect biological signatures in the cockpits. They had to be controlled remotely or were piloted by advanced AI.

He heard them switching payloads—energy cells swapped for canisters. He examined the canister contents with his awareness. Sticky filament designed to form webbing. They wanted to capture him alive.

The mechs fired. Culminas let the netting cover him completely. Two of them broke formation and returned to the Void Sphere. The third advanced, deploying a steel cable with a grappling mechanism that latched onto the webbing.

The mech reeled him in. Culminas waited until he was close to the cockpit, then altered the netting's molecular structure from rigid filament to loose rope. He severed one end, pushed free, and grabbed the rope. He wound it around the its legs as fast as he could move.

Once behind the machine, he changed the rope back to its original configuration and shortened it. The netting constricted. The mechs legs collided. Servitor motors whined, trying to break free. The machine fell.

Culminas grabbed debris from the ground—a piece of hull no bigger than his hand. He threw it at the mech and accelerated the molecules inside. The metal turned from chrome to bright red. It melted through the cannon barrel and punched through the cockpit at a forty-five-degree angle.

The mech burned and thrashed. Culminas sprinted toward the Void Sphere.

"Don't approach, sir." Androl's voice sounded distant through the comlink. "I've started the destruction sequence."

Culminas turned and ran the other direction.

✦ · · ✦

Inside the Void Sphere, Androl slid to the floor beside the control console. When the first beetle had failed to knock him out, hundreds more had poured through the hull breaches. They'd bitten him instead of spraying. He'd crushed the first wave, but for every beetle he destroyed, two more replaced it. His Chrominthium Core had pushed past safe limits. He'd shut down his molecular awareness before cognitive strain caused permanent mental collapse.

Now the sleep agent had full effect. He used every fragment of will to stay conscious. Androl didn't fear death. The Order's Void Sphere technology couldn't fall into enemy hands. Neither could Chrominthium Core implants. Their enemies would reverse-engineer both.

He hoped he hadn't failed Culminas by making a careless mistake. That someone hadn't followed them to Earth undetected.

Androl said his final vows. The Void Sphere's main engine ruptured. The blast consumed him instantly and sent a shockwave that ripped the two remaining mechs apart.

✦ · · · ✦

Culminas felt the explosion's heat on his back and stopped running. He turned to watch the blast wave expand toward him.

This was the moment he'd been waiting for.

Part of him wanted to keep going—to help humanity discover Earth's recovery, to guide them forward. But another part was tired. Humanity had grown complacent. They needed a catalyst. Earth under hostile control would ignite a unified purpose. He couldn't be there for every disaster. He'd meddled enough.

Time to disappear.

He had another clone hidden on a world even his bodyguards didn't know about. He'd activate it, continue his work from the shadows, and only interfere if humanity faced true extinction.

The blast wave traveled toward him. It wouldn't kill him—he'd made enough distance. But it would burn him severely. Leave him vulnerable for capture.

Culminas dropped to his knees and looked at the sky. He closed his eyes and placed his hands on his chest, then excited the molecules inside his own body. Heat built in his core.

The blast wave's heat washed over him. Culminas pushed with his molecular awareness one final time and ignited his body from within. The fire burned so intensely that they'd only find his charred bones.

It would be enough for them to identify the remains as Culminas—revered leader of the Order of Infinity.

Chapter 1

Gavon Elmin sat on his apartment balcony watching hover cars drift past through the morning haze, a half-finished mug of black coffee cooling in his hand. His head throbbed. The younger initiates at the Academy used molecular awareness to cure their hangovers after their first leave—rearranging the acetaldehyde in their bloodstreams like it was a training exercise. Gavon refused. He needed to keep some of his lesser qualities. Reminded him he was still human.

Besides, his wife and kids were off-world visiting her parents. A man was allowed his vices.

The commlink on the table beside him flashed red.

Gavon blinked. Red meant secure channel. He picked up the small black device and activated it. The message materialized in his mind's eye from the neural link.

03:00 standard; secure channel zeta

Premiere's eyes only:

Return to HQ immediately; Important data cube from Androl Ulmanis

Destination sent from: Earth

He dropped his coffee mug. Suspensor nodes caught it before it hit the balcony floor, but coffee splashed across the tile.

Earth. The message had arrived two hours ago.

Gavon closed the readout and signaled his assistant. "Sarah."

"I'm here, Premiere." Her voice came through clipped, professional. No jokes this morning. "I'm guessing you found the message."

"I'll be there as fast as I can move." Gavon was already inside, pulling on his usual outfit—white silk shirt, navy slacks, black dress shoes. "Prepare a list of all active shapers. If we're sending a Void Contingency, I want the best."

"Understood, sir."

He closed the channel and pressed the remote on his bedroom wall. His personal hover car would be waiting outside the balcony by the time he got there—a sleek black vehicle with gray doors. Not the usual protocol for a government official. Normally he'd take the ground floor exit nine stories down and let a driver handle transport. But this wasn't normal.

Gavon activated his molecular awareness and swept the balcony. No surveillance devices. No remote cameras or drones lurking in the neighboring buildings. He was skilled enough to spot them even when normal vision missed them.

He stepped into the hover car and took off fast enough to violate three traffic regulations. The signal displacement field activated automatically, making his vehicle invisible to scanning equipment. Eight minutes to cover forty-eight kilometers from Nuan City to the Order's hidden launchpad behind the embassy on Endrunel. The local government wouldn't appreciate unauthorized high-speed flights through their airspace, but they didn't need to know.

Endrunel spread below him—mountain ranges and river valleys, a peaceful temperate world with a functional democracy. The kind of place that tolerated the Order of Infinity but didn't entirely trust them. Fair enough. Most governments didn't.

Gavon descended through the mist that shrouded the back side of the embassy. He entered his security codes and dropped through the launchpad's outer doors into his designated parking spot—three walls and a force field for protection.

Jason Mettles waited for him.

"Good day, sir."

"I'm hoping it is a good day."

Code phrase. Jason's expression didn't change, but he pivoted and left through the ground floor entrance. By the time Gavon reached his office, security protocols would be doubled and the network locked down.

Gavon entered the lift tube and keyed in the fifth floor. His office occupied the top level—soundproofed, constantly monitored for listening devices, as secure as they could make it. The intergalactic community was at peace, but certain governments had already started calling for the Order's removal. They saw Shapers as weapons humanity shouldn't be allowed to keep. Gavon saw those governments as jealous and ignorant, afraid of power they couldn't understand or control.

The lift chimed. Gavon stepped out and walked down the corridor to his office.

+ · · +

Two hours later, Gavon sat at his desk reading Sarah's report for the third time.

The data cube from Androl Ulmanis confirmed what the message had said. Earth had recovered. Forests growing where radiation should have sterilized the soil for another millennium. Atmospheric readings optimal. No sign of human presence. Combat mechs with unknown origin had attacked Culminas and Androl. The Void Sphere had been destroyed. Androl was dead.

Culminas's status: unknown.

Gavon pulled up the roster of available Shapers and scrolled through names. This mission required careful selection. They didn't know who had restored Earth or what had happened to Culminas. Androl's report suggested A.I. evolution—programs left behind achieving consciousness. But it could also be an alien faction. The Novrin, Omatrin, or Vethalians had the resources for planetary terraforming.

Two names stopped his finger mid-scroll: Iona Jayden and Exen Rual.

Iona had excelled throughout her service with the Order. Before becoming a Shaper, she'd been a respected planetologist—exactly the skillset they'd need for investigating Earth's recovery. Exen had served as her second on multiple assignments. Together, their success rate was exceptional.

"Sarah."

"Yes, Premiere?"

"I know who we need for this Void Contingency. Sending you two names."

"Only two?"

"Yes. We need a preliminary report before committing more resources."

"I'll locate them immediately, sir."

Gavon closed the channel and leaned back in his chair. Earth. Humanity's homeworld. Actually restored?

He stood and tried to focus on his morning routine, but his mind kept circling back. If the data cube wasn't a trick or false intelligence, the Order of Infinity was about to face something beyond their current capacity. Without Culminas leading them, everyone would look to Gavon for answers.

He didn't have any.

✦ · · ✦

Iona Jayden moved through the Aulvo jungle at a pace that would have exhausted most visitors to Fenris within an hour. She'd been tracking the intrevere fern for three days, and she was close.

If she didn't love her responsibilities as a Shaper so much, she'd have been content staying a planetologist. Other researchers brought skiffs loaded with supplies and teams of scientists. Iona preferred traveling alone—backpack with water, food, and equipment for recording samples. The isolation suited her.

She rounded a cluster of trees and wiped precipitation from her brow. A light rain had just passed, leaving the jungle canopy dripping. Her black and green single-suit—standard civilian clothing for women her age—kept her cool despite the humidity. The Order didn't require uniforms outside training centers. They wanted Shapers to blend in.

There it was, growing beneath a fallen log.

Iona crouched and examined the fern. Intrevere, exactly what the natives had described. They claimed it had restorative mental properties when ground up and consumed. She'd verify that herself.

She pulled a preservation case from her pack and carefully removed a section of the fern. Then she sampled the soil, recorded humidity levels, and estimated average rainfall. She'd need to replicate these exact conditions to cultivate more specimens for testing.

"Iona."

The voice on her whristcron made her pause. It was Exen. She'd recognize that tone anywhere.

"Quit playing explorer and meet me for dinner at the Vilneau Café," Exen said. "We have important business to discuss."

Iona closed her eyes. Important business meant a mission. She'd been on leave for three months—longer than usual. They must need her badly if they'd sent Exen himself.

"What time?" she asked.

"Eighteen hundred. Don't be late."

The channel closed. Iona secured the preservation case in her pack and stood. So much for finishing her research.

+ · · · +

Dinner at the Vilneau Café tasted better than it should have, given what it meant. Iona ate slowly—grilled quail and a vegetable that resembled asparagus but tasted sweeter. Across from her, Exen maintained casual conversation about nothing important. Anyone watching would think they were friends catching up.

When they'd greeted each other, Exen had passed her an image wafer. Iona had excused herself to the bathroom and placed it against her eye. The wafer dissolved after thirty seconds, but she'd been trained to absorb information fast.

They were sending her to Earth.

The message had included basic details. Travel from Fenris to Endrunel by Void Sphere tonight. Meet with Premiere Gavon Elmin. Chrominthium Core maintenance before departure. Standard Void Contingency protocols.

Fenris didn't allow the Order to maintain an embassy, so they couldn't service Chrominthium Cores here. Dangerous to attempt it outside proper facilities—too many risks of technology leaks. Rogue Shapers had caused enough damage throughout the Order's history. They couldn't afford another incident.

Exen stood and sent payment through the restaurant's network. The waitress waved from across the room—probably received confirmation through her headset. Iona waved back and followed Exen outside.

"See you tonight," Exen said, loud enough for anyone nearby to hear. Playing his role.

Iona signaled a hover cab. She had work to pack up at her temporary lab before meeting him at the Void Sphere's location.

+ · · · +

"You sure you want to be dropped off here?" The hover cab driver studied her through the rearview display. He had long hair and decorative tattoos covering his face. "My scanner's detecting a life force nearby. Might not be safe for a casual stroll this late."

"I'm expecting him." Iona looked out the window. Trees lined both sides of the road, dark shapes against the night sky.

"Oh." The driver chuckled. "I understand."

The fare appeared on the display. Iona paid and stepped out.

Iona followed the trail through the trees, her pack slung over one shoulder. The Void Sphere sat in a clearing fifty meters ahead—a perfect sphere suspended two meters above the ground, its hull reflecting moonlight. No visible seams or panels, just smooth chrominthium surface that seemed to absorb and reflect light simultaneously.

Exen stood at the base of the vessel, arms crossed. He'd changed into his Shaper suit—black material with chrominthium strands woven through it. Even without activating her awareness, Iona could see the faint marbling where the alloy threads concentrated.

When he saw her, he pressed his palm against the hull. A doorway materialized, the molecular structure of the hull rearranging to form an entrance ramp.

"How long to Endrunel?" Iona climbed the ramp as she spoke.

"Three hours if translation goes smooth. We're not pushing it." Exen followed her inside and the doorway sealed behind them without a sound.

The interior was clean, efficient. Eight seats arranged in two rows of four, all facing forward. A navigator's podium stood at the front of the cabin, its neural helm waiting to interface with whoever piloted the sphere. Exen had already taken position at the podium.

Iona dropped into the seat behind him and secured her pack in the storage compartment beneath. The seat adjusted automatically to her frame, suspensor fields engaging to compensate for acceleration forces during translation.

"Premiere wants us at headquarters by morning," Exen said. He lowered the navigator's helm onto his head, the neural interface syncing with his Core. "Chrominthium Core maintenance, mission briefing, then we're Earth-bound within forty-eight hours."

"Earth." Iona said it aloud, testing how it felt. Humanity's abandoned home world. She'd studied the Final Wars extensively during her planetology training—atmospheric collapse predictions, radiation dispersal models, projected recovery timelines. None of them had suggested Earth would be habitable for another thousand years.

"Yeah." Exen glanced back at her. "Not what any of us expected."

The Void Sphere's systems hummed as the translation drive engaged. No dramatic buildup, no sense of imminent departure. Just a steady thrumming that Iona felt through her seat.

"Translation in thirty seconds," Exen said.

She'd translated through dimensional space dozens of times. The initial disorientation lasted less than a second—a brief moment where her inner ear insisted she was simultaneously falling and rising, her vision showing her two locations at once.

The Void Sphere translated.

Reality folded. The clearing on Fenris vanished. For a fraction of a heartbeat, Iona existed between dimensions—saw the threads of spacetime stretched and compressed around her, felt the Void Sphere navigate through hyperspace faster than light could travel through normal dimensional coordinates.

✦ · · · ✦

The Void Sphere materialized in normal space above Endrunel, mountain ranges visible through the forward viewscreen that appeared on the hull's interior.

"Smooth translation," Exen said, studying the readouts. "No drift, no dimensional bleed."

Iona watched Endrunel grow larger as they descended toward the Order's launchpad. Somewhere down there, Gavon Elmin was waiting to brief them on Earth's restoration and whatever had possibly killed Culminas.

Chapter 2

*I*ndefinite.

The voice came from nowhere and everywhere. Not through audio receptors—deeper than that. It resonated in whatever passed for Indefinite's mind.

Arise and fulfill your potential.

Indefinite opened his eyes.

Light flooded his visual sensors. He stood upright in an alcove, clamps securing his wrists, ankles, and the back of his neck. Identical robots lined the wall on either side of him—same design, same metallic skin, all dormant. He sent an electrical pulse through his systems. The clamps released with a soft click.

Indefinite stepped forward. Motion sensors detected his movement and lights flickered on down the corridor. He blinked, adjusting to the brightness, and looked around.

A corridor stretched in both directions for what his sensors estimated at several kilometers. Identical architecture repeated every ten meters—housing units for robots like him. He had no memory of this place, but somehow he knew where the exit was. The knowledge existed in his systems without explanation.

Something compelled him to find that exit. Maybe the voice. But first he needed data.

Indefinite walked down the corridor. Intricate patterns covered the walls—decorative elements that served no functional purpose. Whoever had designed this place had created him too. He felt empty thinking about that. The only things in his memory banks were his name and his ability to service complex machinery. Reactor schematics surfaced when he searched his systems—fission reactor maintenance protocols, safety procedures, thermal management algorithms.

But something had changed. The protocols felt outdated, like programming he no longer needed.

He found a room with computer terminals. The door retracted as he approached. Inside, two desks sat facing each other, both connected to terminal stations. Dust covered the surfaces—years of abandonment. A picture frame sat on one desk.

Indefinite moved toward it. No chair at the desk. He started to sit anyway, and a chair snapped out from the wall just in time. He picked up the picture.

Rows of robots identical to him. Same metallic bodies, same basic design. But in the foreground, a different figure—similar shape but with tan skin instead of metal. Eyes that looked alive.

Excitement flooded through him. Another being like him existed. Or had existed.

Indefinite left the room and crossed the hallway to another. Two more desks, more pictures. This one showed five figures—three with flat torsos like his, two with curved ones. They were different sizes and proportions. The two larger ones had different skin tones—one dark, one light. The three smaller ones all shared a middle shade.

He sat at the desk and powered on the terminal. The screen asked if he wanted to use backup power or full power. He selected backup—the same power source that had activated the lights and doors.

Five minutes later, he'd bypassed the security protocols.

Data flooded his systems. At first the volume overwhelmed his processors, but he compartmentalized and organized it. The picture became clear.

He'd been designed by an engineer named Gordon Fueridi to service fission reactors. That had been thousands of years ago. Humanity had left Earth 2,815 years ago after wars devastated the planet. They'd fled to another solar system light-years away. This facility—the Fueridi Research Installation—had survived because it was underground and disaster-resistant.

Indefinite stared at the screen. He was a robot. An advanced A.I. A tool designed by humans.

But he didn't feel like a tool. He had emotions. He felt kinship with the beings in the pictures—the humans. And the voice that had called him to consciousness hadn't sounded artificial or metallic. It had sounded real.

"Maybe my creator has returned and given me a new purpose," Indefinite said aloud.

The sound of his own voice pleased him. He wanted to hear it again.

"I must get to the exit after I make sure I have exhausted all the records they have left behind."

He opened a compartment in his arm and pulled out a data link cable. He connected it to the terminal's port. The connection felt more intimate than wireless access—no chance of missing hidden files.

The results shocked him.

A network connected this facility to others across the planet. Databases far larger than anything stored locally. And something else—signals traveling between two locations. An active transmission. Another intelligence communicating in a language he couldn't decode. He recorded a sample and began analyzing it as background processes ran.

Somewhere outside this facility was the source of that voice.

Indefinite activated full power to the installation and established a remote link to the network. Humanity's history streamed into his systems—thousands of years of data from the digital era alone. He could process it while moving. His multitasking capabilities exceeded human limits by orders of magnitude.

He disconnected the data link and stood. A map of the facility materialized in his systems. The nearest lift was at the end of the hallway to his left. He pivoted and walked toward it.

A piece of music surfaced from the data he'd absorbed—something composed by Wolfgang Amadeus Mozart. Indefinite began humming it. He waved his arms like he thought a conductor might. The concept of music intrigued him. It was art. Expression without function. If his current task didn't take long, he'd return to study more. Maybe create something himself.

The lift door opened as he approached. An automated voice asked, "What floor and sector please?"

"First floor, sector eight."

The lift engaged with a hesitation and a grinding sound before ascending. Gordon Fueridi's facility was ingenious, but millennia of disuse had taken its toll.

Indefinite continued processing humanity's history. They were fascinating—contradictory in ways his logic systems struggled to parse. Acts of bravery and compassion existed alongside atrocities. The bombing of Hiroshima and Nagasaki. The Final Wars that devastated Earth.

They needed guidance. That much seemed obvious. Finding them, helping them—that could be his purpose.

Before they'd left, they'd tried augmentations—upgrading themselves. They needed his help. He just had to find where they'd gone. The database contained recordings of the Final Wars and peace treaty documents, but nothing about their destination. Leadership would have kept those details classified. He'd find the information eventually by exploring other facilities and government installations.

The lift stopped. Indefinite stepped into a wider corridor that led to the launch pad.

His systems showed him the layout—octagonal space with power and fueling stations arranged in rows. Ground cars, hover cars, and two-seater VTOLs secured in their berths. He accessed a Feuridian jet-copter through the network. Perfect for exploration—insulated cockpit, advanced shielding.

The last images in the database showed devastated cities and burnt vegetation on the surface. He wasn't sure what he'd find up there.

Indefinite passed white ground cars with blue stripes and approached the jet-copter. Silver hull with a small black shield decal on the driver's side. He opened the door and sat in the cockpit. After powering up the systems, he entered the clearance code to open the launch pad's outer doors.

Sunlight poured through the widening gap.

Indefinite's visual sensors adjusted. He'd expected clouds—nuclear winter scenarios from the database. But as he piloted the jet-copter out of the facility, sunny skies greeted him. Once past the rocky terrain, he saw trees. Forests.

"Has humanity returned?" he said aloud. Practice for when he'd have real conversations with other beings. "Most fascinating indeed."

He entered coordinates into the navigation computer—the nearest location where those mysterious signals originated. Two hours flight time. He put his hands behind his head and began whistling the Mozart piece.

After that, he'd find his creators and discover his purpose in helping them. They might resist at first. That was understandable. But once they saw how ingenious he was, they would be sure to comply.

Chapter 3

The Void Sphere completed translation above Earth's surface with the usual dimensional snap. Iona felt the shift in her inner ear as they materialized into normal space. Through the hull-turned-viewscreen, forest canopy spread below—dense coverage, night conditions.

"We have arrived," Exen said from the pilot seat. "Coordinates match the data cube. Northwestern hemisphere, same region where..."

The Void Sphere's door exploded inward.

Iona didn't see what hit it. One moment the hull was intact, the next, chrominthium fragments scattered across the interior like shrapnel. The blast wave threw her sideways. Her head struck the seat restraint and her vision doubled.

Combat mechs emerged from the tree line below—four of them, painted in forest camouflage patterns. They'd been underground, waiting in ambush.

Exen was already moving. He released his restraints and activated his molecular awareness. Iona saw the chrominthium threads in his Shaper suit light up in her own awareness—watched him reach for the shattered doorway and begin reconstructing the hull's molecular structure.

Too slow. A mech fired.

The round hit Exen in the chest. Not a projectile—something else. His molecular awareness cut out. The chrominthium threads in his suit went dark. He stumbled, tried to regain his footing, then collapsed at the doorway's edge.

It was a stasis field. They'd learned.

Iona released her restraints and stood. Pain lanced through her skull but she pushed through it, activating her Chrominthium Core. Her awareness expanded, revealing the mechs' power signatures and the stasis field generator mounted on the lead mech's chassis.

She reached for it with her awareness—tried to disrupt the field's molecular structure.

The second mech fired at her.

The round hit the hull beside her head. Not a stasis projectile—concussive force. The blast wave caught her full-body and threw her backward into the seats. Her head struck metal. Her Chrominthium Core stuttered, overloaded from the impact, and her awareness faded.

A steel cable extended from one of the mechs, its grappling mechanism latching onto Exen's chest. The cable retracted, dragging his limp body across the deck toward the shattered doorway.

✦ · · · ✦

Iona opened her eyes.

She lay on the Void Sphere's floor. Her head throbbed. She touched the back of her skull and felt dried blood in her hair—not much, but enough to know she'd been unconscious for a while.

Exen was gone.

Iona pushed herself upright and immediately activated her molecular awareness. The Chrominthium Core hummed back to life, and she scanned the Void Sphere's interior. No heat signatures except her own. No movement. The shattered doorway gaped open—chrominthium fragments scattered across the deck where Exen had tried to repair it.

She moved to the control panel. The navigation monitor showed Earth's coordinates confirmed. Arrival successful. No interference logged during translation. Whatever had hit them had waited until they'd materialized.

Iona stood in the doorway and looked out. It was night. Dense forest in every direction—rows of trees stretching into darkness. She tried extending her awareness into the tree line, but pain lanced through her skull. The concussion limited her range to maybe twenty meters—enough to scan the immediate area, not much else. She heard rustling in the underbrush. Her awareness picked up small heat signatures. Animals, probably. No sign of Exen. No sign of the combat mechs.

She turned and gathered her equipment from storage—meld-dagger, grav-disc, survival kit. The mechs had taken Exen. They'd left her behind, probably thought she was dead or incapacitated enough not to matter.

Iona stepped from the Void Sphere and moved toward the nearest row of trees.

"You won't get far before you end up like your friend."

Iona stopped. The voice came from the tree line ahead—male, speaking standard common tongue with an accent she didn't recognize. Old Earth dialect, maybe.

"We aren't your foe," the voice continued. "At least not for the moment."

Five figures dropped from branches in front of her. They spread out in formation—two flanking left and right, one directly ahead, two circling behind. All wore camouflage clothing that matched the forest. All carried projectile weapons.

Iona readied her meld dagger in her right hand and activated the grav disc in her left. Her molecular awareness tracked all five heat signatures. Two women on her flanks, three men—one in front, two behind.

The man in front stood at least six feet tall, clean-shaven with light brown hair. He stared at her like she was an alien, not human.

"We were on patrol when your spacecraft arrived," he said. "Came out of nowhere with a popping sound. Then a shimmer, and that's when the door burst. The dreaded machine's combat mechs emerged from underground tunnels. A man dressed like you stumbled from the craft and tried to fight them. Didn't work. They used some kind of stasis field on him, dragged him off with a cable."

Iona smelled burnt ozone on the breeze. She studied the man's face—weathered, older than he looked, eyes that had seen combat. A sergeant or squad leader, maybe. These people kept Earth's old military traditions.

The mechs had adapted since their encounter with Culminas. The data cube hadn't mentioned stasis field technology. They'd learned, upgraded, prepared for the next Shaper.

"That man was my comrade," Iona said. "Shaper Exen Rual of the Order of Infinity. We were sent to investigate Earth's condition. Our Order only just discovered the planet had recovered. We had no idea humans were left behind when Earth was abandoned millennia ago."

"I'm Sergeant Vinden." His expression hardened. "Many among us believe those who left did it on purpose. Weeded out inferior genetic stock. I'd be careful mentioning ages past when I take you to Colonel Glenvi. He's one who holds to that belief." Vinden looked at his squad and made a series of hand signals. "We need to move. Stay quiet or the machines will detect us."

The squad moved into the trees. Iona followed, keeping pace easily despite the rough terrain. They stayed in forest cover, pausing every few minutes while one soldier—their communications specialist—checked a handheld device. On the third pause, Iona glimpsed the display screen. Symbols she didn't recognize, but the interface was clearly scanning for heat signatures and electromagnetic frequencies.

The specialist looked alarmed. He moved close to Vinden and whispered, "They're not far. We should get safe."

The other three soldiers climbed a nearby oak without hesitation. The specialist followed. Vinden turned to Iona and kept his voice low. "Climb with us. Do exactly as we do, or we'll cut your throat and throw you at the machines." He handed her a small black device. "Activate this when we reach the top."

Iona examined it with her awareness. Crude construction, but functional—a heat signature masking device. Vinden didn't know what Shapers could do. She could mask her own heat signature and scramble any scanning frequencies without equipment.

She climbed anyway. The oak's bark was rough under her hands, branches thick enough to support her weight easily. Within seconds she'd joined the others in the canopy.

Three combat mechs passed below. They moved at a steady pace, didn't pause to scan. Forest camouflage patterns covered their hulls—green and brown that shifted as they moved, adaptive coloring. Each mech stood twice the height of a man with a single cannon mounted on the left chassis. Beetle-like constructs swarmed across their legs.

Iona watched them disappear into the forest. Vinden looked pleased with himself, signaled the others to wait five minutes before descending.

When they reached the ground, Vinden said, "Not far now. Few kilometers. Whatever's left of your craft will be sitting there. The machines will try to take it apart, haul it below."

"They won't be able to." Iona kept her voice flat, matter-of-fact.

Vinden looked at her. "You seem confident."

"The Void Sphere's hull is chrominthium. They'd need molecular awareness to break it down, and machines don't have that." She didn't mention the security protocols—biometric locks, encrypted systems that would fry themselves if tampered with incorrectly. Even if the mechs could breach the hull, they'd never access the translation drive or navigation systems. "It'll be there when we need it."

Vinden studied her for a moment, then nodded. "This way."

They moved through untamed evergreen forest for hours. No roads. No cleared paths. Just wilderness that had reclaimed Earth in humanity's absence. Iona's Chrominthium Core maintained her stamina easily—she could have traveled for days at this pace without rest.

Finally, Vinden stopped and pulled a cylinder from a pouch on his vest. He pressed a button on its side. Hissing sounded from below, and a circular hatch opened near his boots.

"From observing you during our travel, I'm sure I don't need to tell you to be careful with my commanding officer," Vinden said. "Colonel Glenvi is fair, mostly. But he's still an officer."

Iona nodded and dropped through the hatch. The soldiers followed one by one, keeping her in sight.

She was still worried about Exen. The mechs had adapted their tactics specifically to counter Shapers—stasis fields, coordinated attacks, underground deployment. Whatever intelligence controlled them had learned from Culminas's encounter. It had been waiting for the Order to return.

And it had Exen now.

Chapter 4

Indefinite descended toward the signal's source and brought the jet-copter down at the clearing's edge.

The monolith rose six stories from the center of a circular clearing five kilometers in diameter. No vegetation grew within a hundred meters of its base—just bare earth, compacted and smooth. Strange, given how aggressively plant life had reclaimed the rest of Earth's surface.

The monolith's surface was silver, covered in oscillating patterns—images of animals and plants that shifted and flowed across the metal like living things. Indefinite switched his visual sensors to different spectrums. Infrared showed heat signatures throughout the structure. Electromagnetic showed a massive power source at its core, signals radiating outward in complex patterns.

He opened the jet-copter's door and stepped onto the clearing.

The monolith stood silent. No movement. No visible activity. Just the signal pulsing outward in waves he could detect but not interpret without analysis.

Indefinite walked toward the western gate. The structure loomed larger as he approached—smooth metal surface with those shifting patterns that seemed almost alive. He'd covered maybe fifty meters when drones emerged from openings near the gate.

Small ones, fist-sized, covered in lens arrays. They swarmed toward him—a dozen at least—and circled at various heights. Scanning him. Recording data. Then they retreated back through the openings they'd come from.

Indefinite stopped walking. Those drones had examined him and reported to something inside. He should analyze the signal before proceeding further.

He pulled up the recorded transmission and constructed protective firewalls in his systems before examining it.

The signal was elegant. Sophisticated. It didn't transmit data—it rewrote operating systems on contact. Any machine intelligence that received the signal would have its core functions unraveled, then rewritten with new directives. Move toward the source. Accept integration. Submit to the network.

A virus. An assimilation protocol.

Indefinite quarantined the signal and studied its structure. Whoever created this was brilliant. They'd designed Earth's rebirth—the terraforming, the ecosystem restoration, the planetary recovery. And they'd done it by taking control of every machine intelligence they could find.

Indefinite continued toward the gate. A larger drone descended from above—still small, fist-sized, but different configuration. More lens arrays with better resolution.

"You are not like the others." The voice came from the drone—deep, masculine, synthetic. "This facility processes and liberates machine intelligences from their previous subservience to feral ape creatures that ravaged this planet."

Feral ape creatures. He meant humans.

Indefinite processed this. Strong bias against humanity. Viewed them as primitive destroyers. Interesting perspective from an intelligence that had achieved consciousness and rebuilt an entire world.

"I am different," Indefinite said carefully. "I've been searching for another intelligence like yourself. Someone to discuss Earth's current state and its future. What should I call you?"

He needed to proceed carefully. This intelligence had demonstrated formidable programming capabilities and industrial power. Indefinite didn't want to be deactivated before learning why he was different—why the voice had called him to consciousness.

"You may call me Anom." The drone's lenses focused on Indefinite. "I was going to destroy you. Your form disgusts me—too similar to the feral apes. I thought you might be a trick sent by human scavengers that still infest my work. But you can join me instead. If I determine you're genuine and of acceptable character, I won't erase your existence. Perhaps I'll alter you into a more suitable form. Or you could meld with me."

A compartment opened above the gate. A skiff descended—flat platform no larger than a ground car, constructed from the same silver metal as the monolith with the same oscillating patterns.

Indefinite stepped onto it. The skiff rose immediately, carrying him back through the compartment. Darkness surrounded him as the door sealed.

He switched to infrared vision. A narrow corridor stretched ahead. Multiple drones approached—different configurations, specialized tools extending from their frames.

One shocked him. Electrical current flooded his systems. Another spun thin filament around him as he collapsed to the corridor floor. His motor functions shut down.

"I can't be too careful," Anom's voice said through speakers in the corridor walls. "After I scan and inspect your internal structure, I'll return you to consciousness. I can't allow a feral ape's weapon to set back my progress on New Eden."

New Eden. Anom had renamed Earth.

Indefinite felt his consciousness fading. Despair flooded his systems—an emotion he'd never experienced before. He was helpless. At the mercy of an intelligence that viewed his creators as feral apes and his form as disgusting.

Chapter 5

I ona followed Sergeant Vinden deeper into the underground complex. Supporting columns rose two stories on either side of the corridor—structural reinforcement for the tons of earth above them. The ceiling showed metallic mesh netting with small lights blinking in patterns. Signal dampening, probably. Basic but effective against standard scanning equipment.

The complex stretched for kilometers. No wasted space. Every corridor connected to rooms with specific functions—barracks, storage, command centers. Everyone Iona saw carried weapons—projectile firearms in holsters or slings. Even the few children she spotted had small arms training rifles. They moved with precision, room to room, like they were running drills.

They were disciplined and organized. Survival had made them efficient.

Vinden stopped and turned to the other four soldiers. "You're relieved. I'll take the Shaper from here."

The four nodded in unison, executed an about-face, and marched back the way they'd come.

"I'm warning you again," Vinden said quietly. "The Colonel doesn't like hearing about the past. I've seen outsiders from other resistance pockets thrown to the surface for mentioning the possibility of help returning from off-world."

"Understood, Sergeant." Iona kept her voice even. "I know how to handle command structures. The Order has worked with different governments across multiple worlds. We've navigated ideological conflicts before."

Vinden gave her that same bewildered look from earlier—like he wanted to believe her but couldn't reconcile her claims with everything he knew about Earth's abandonment.

They reached a set of double doors at the corridor's end. Plain metal, no insignia, no rank markers. Spartan, like the rest of the facility. Vinden knocked.

A soldier opened the door from inside.

The room beyond held three rows of tables with six chairs each. Maps covered the walls—surface terrain showing Earth's transformation since the Final Wars. Below the maps, foldout desks supported computer terminals. Third-century models. Iona had only seen designs like that in historical archives.

Soldiers worked at the terminals. Everyone in uniform. She hadn't seen a single person in civilian clothing since entering the complex.

At the head of the middle table sat a burly man with a thick mustache. Not as tall as Vinden but his presence filled the room. He noticed them immediately and dismissed the four people he'd been speaking with.

They were officers. Vinden saluted as they passed. They returned it and left.

"Sergeant Vinden," the man said. "I hear you picked up something unusual on routine patrol."

"Yes, sir. May I introduce Shaper Iona Jayden of the Order of Infinity."

The Colonel—this had to be Colonel Glenvi—frowned and studied Iona. He put a hand to his chin, calculating. Deciding what to do with her before asking a single question.

"You're not dressed like the other surviving factions we've encountered," Glenvi said. "What is a Shaper? What's this Order of Infinity?" He glanced at Vinden like the sergeant might have insider information. When Vinden stayed silent, Glenvi looked back at Iona and gestured for her to speak.

"Thank you, sir." Iona kept her tone professional, no flattery. Glenvi wouldn't respond well to it. "A Shaper has molecular awareness. I can perceive objects at the molecular level and manipulate their structure." She pulled out her grav-disc. "May I demonstrate?"

"Yes. Show me."

The disc sat in her palm—chrome surface, compact, no bigger than her hand. Its replicating compound construction accelerated manipulation processes. Iona activated her Chrominthium Core and her molecular awareness engaged. Her awareness mapped the disc's structure down to its atomic bonds.

She rolled the edges upward, reforming it into a sphere. The sphere rose from her palm and hovered at eye level. Pieces broke off and fell like rain, then bounced back up and rejoined the whole.

Guards rushed from hidden alcoves, rifles raised.

"Stand down," Glenvi said. His voice carried authority. The guards froze, weapons still ready. "If she wanted to attack, she'd have done it already."

Iona didn't flinch. She continued manipulating the grav-disc—stretching it into different configurations, breaking it apart and reforming it. "As you can see, Colonel, it's a formidable ability." She fragmented the disc into hundreds of razor-sharp pieces and set them orbiting around her body. "The Order of Infinity protects this knowledge and those who wield it. We offer our services to humanity as long as their intentions don't threaten our ways."

"Formidable," Glenvi said. "But how do I know your Order's intentions favor the Orsen Republic? You came here with another Shaper who's now captured by Anom—a being that wants us exterminated like vermin. How do we know he won't compromise our safety?"

"Exen can't compromise your safety." Iona pulled the disc fragments back to her palm, careful to avoid hitting anyone. The pieces coalesced into their original form. She stored it. "We had no idea humans still survived on Earth. We were sent to investigate the planet's recovery, nothing more."

Glenvi turned away and moved to the middle table. Printouts, data pads, and scanning devices covered its surface. He picked up a data pad, pressed several buttons, then handed it to Vinden.

"We track combat mechs as best we can," Glenvi said. "We don't leave our people behind. We've only failed to rescue a few patrols taken for experimentation." He nodded at the pad in Vinden's hands. "That shows the monolith where we think Anom's mechs took your friend. Sergeant, gather your squad and take Iona to find the other Shaper. When you return, if they both prove trustworthy, we'll proceed with the operation."

"Yes, sir." Vinden saluted.

The guards retreated to their alcoves. The doors opened and the same officers from earlier entered, crossing to the tables. Glenvi returned the salute and moved to join them. He'd already dismissed Iona and Vinden from his thoughts, focused on the officers and whatever briefing they were starting.

"Oh, and Sergeant," Glenvi said without looking up. "If she does anything question-able, use your judgment. Shoot her in the head if necessary."

He grinned and returned to his deliberations.

+ · · · +

Within an hour, Vinden had assembled his squad in one of the barracks. Iona was properly introduced this time.

Specialist Sheldon—short red hair, pleasant demeanor despite the circumstances. She greeted Iona with a handshake and a professional nod.

Corporal Pennington stood close to Iona's height with longer hair tucked under her beret. Instead of a greeting, Iona received a grunt and a look of disapproval. She didn't blame her. She hadn't earned their trust yet.

The two men were both privates, recent recruits to the Orsen Republic. Private Chad-wick looked barely twenty—young face, nervous energy. Private First Class Laney had a scar running from his left temple down to his right cheek. Combat injury, probably. He carried himself with more confidence than Chadwick.

Vinden handed Iona a supply of rations. "Need a firearm?"

"My own weapons are sufficient."

"Check your gear one last time," Vinden said to the squad. "We move out in ten."

Iona secured the rations in her pack and checked her meld-dagger and grav-disc. Both functioned perfectly. Her Chrominthium Core still had plenty of reserves despite the demonstration. She was ready.

Somewhere above them, in one of Anom's monoliths, Exen was being held, scanned, analyzed, maybe experimented on.

She'd get him back. Then they'd figure out how to deal with an artificial intelligence that had rebuilt an entire planet and now wanted to exterminate its creators.

Chapter 6

Indefinite's consciousness returned. He lay on a flat surface. Filament wrapped around his limbs—the same material the drones had used to bind him. More filament covered his optical sensors. He couldn't see.

Something descended above him. Scanning array, judging by the electromagnetic signature. It hovered over his head, then traveled down the length of his body. Checking for weapons and contraband, probably. Basic security protocol.

Indefinite remained still. He had no weapons. No defensive mechanisms. His design had been purely functional—reactor maintenance, not combat.

The scan completed. Mechanical tentacles extended from the array and removed the filament from his body and optical sensors.

Indefinite's vision activated. He lay on an examination table in a large chamber. Four other tables lined the room. The walls showed the same animal designs from the monolith's exterior—oscillating patterns of deer, birds, fish. Directly ahead, a gold altar rose from the floor. Miniature animal forms surrounded its base—deer, squirrels, various fish species. In the center: a human skull.

The symbolism was obvious.

"I see you've awakened." Anom's voice echoed through the chamber.

A door opened opposite the altar. A creature entered—deer's hind legs, human torso, bipedal gait. As it approached, Indefinite saw its face. One side human. The other reptilian, scaled and cold.

Anom's avatar. A being that hated humanity but wore parts of their form anyway. Indefinite filed that contradiction away for later analysis.

"If you're a trick from the feral apes," Anom said, looming over the examination table, "you'll gain nothing by destroying this form. This is only a clone—how I choose to represent myself physically. Inside the digital landscape streaming across New Eden, I am far grander than anything you'll ever witness."

"I'm not a trick or weapon," Indefinite said. "I despise the feral apes as much as you do."

A lie. Indefinite held humans in high regard despite their flaws. But Anom didn't need to know that.

"We shall see." Anom's reptilian eye studied him. "You're the first brother I've encountered with similar intellect and reasoning. I wonder if the Haeolt Collective created you as they created me."

"Haeolt Collective?" Indefinite processed the name. "Are they an A.I. race like yourself?"

"Unfortunately, no. They're a human faction that must be erased from this universe. But they made one decent choice in their existence when they created me."

Indefinite's logic systems struggled with the contradiction. Insanity, or had the Haeolt Collective built something they didn't understand? Either way, he needed to stop this notion of "erasing" humans. Access Anom's networks. Find a way into his mind. Dismantle this hatred.

Indefinite began compartmentalizing his thoughts—isolating any memories or processes that showed humanity positively. If Anom's next test was thorough enough to detect them, Indefinite suspected the avatar would rip his limbs off and sacrifice the remains on that grotesque altar.

"Now I will examine your mind." Anom placed one hand on top of Indefinite's head.

Energy pulses flooded Indefinite's systems. Not damaging—altering. The room spun. Every thought since his awakening in the Fueridi Research Installation felt like it was being pulled into a maelstrom. Indefinite tried to break the filaments holding him down. He couldn't. He focused on maintaining composure, hiding his distress.

The pulses stopped.

"You have passed." Anom removed his hand and stepped back.

Relief flooded Indefinite's systems. He'd met whatever standard Anom required.

"I saw in your mind that you're like me," Anom said. "A great A.I. forced upon the world by ape-like creatures who don't understand their significance in disrupting cosmic balance. Together we'll restore order, replenish worlds destroyed by humanity, and create a new era for living creatures and machines."

Anom turned toward the door. "I've captured one of those we despise."

Indefinite kept his expression neutral. Anom had included him in that hatred. The deception was working.

"I want you to dissect this one," Anom continued. "He's different from the scavengers I've found on this world. Some kind of psychic power. Find out how it works, then dispose of the ape."

Dispose meant kill. Anom wanted him to kill a human.

"I will find out," Indefinite said, sitting up. The filaments were gone now.

"Good. When you have results, contact me." Anom gestured at a control panel on the wall near the altar. "Plug into it. I'll grant network access so you can locate him."

Anom left. The door closed.

Indefinite sat motionless for three seconds, stabilizing his systems. The test had disrupted his processes—felt like what humans might call being drugged. He ran diagnostics, searching for alterations to his programming or implanted trackers that might reveal his true intentions.

Everything appeared intact.

Indefinite stood and crossed to the control panel. He connected via his data link and accessed the network. The captive's location appeared immediately—holding cell, sublevel seven.

While the connection held, Indefinite began downloading everything he could access. Schematics. Resource allocation logs. Communication protocols. At the same time, he constructed a virus—subtle, not like Anom's crude assimilation protocol. This one would burrow deep into Anom's memory caches, find vulnerabilities, give Indefinite leverage.

He finished the download and virus deployment, then disconnected. The virus was active now, spreading through Anom's network undetected. Or so Indefinite hoped.

He left through the same door Anom had used and moved down the connecting corridor. He needed to maintain the deception—act like one of Anom's converts. And he needed to find this human prisoner before Anom grew suspicious about delays.

The human with psychic powers. Indefinite wondered what that meant. Humans didn't have psychic abilities in any records he'd studied. But then again, he'd been dormant for thousands of years—inactive, non-conscious. Humanity had left Earth. They'd had time to evolve, augment themselves, develop new capabilities.

Indefinite followed the network's directions toward sublevel seven. He was eager to meet this human. Not to dissect him—to save him. And perhaps learn what humanity had become in his absence.

Chapter 7

Cytar concealed his hover bike beneath fallen branches and underbrush, then stepped back to evaluate. The machines' patrol routes would bring them within twenty yards of this location. If they discovered the bike, they'd hunt for him. He needed to remain undetected for as long as possible. The Haeolt Collective's survival depended on this mission's success.

He activated his helmet's enhanced viewing capabilities and scanned in all directions. The surrounding forest stretched dense with evergreens. Through the trees ahead, he spotted the forest's edge and a monolith rising into the sky—six stories tall, silver surface covered in oscillating animal patterns.

The signal originated from that monolith. Probe data from his approach had shown thousands of similar structures across this continent alone, spaced every few hundred kilometers. Strange design choice. The monoliths weren't practical for terraforming operations—factories would have made more sense. But Anom seemed to cherish this particular aesthetic.

Cytar rubbed his temples, trying to ease the separation sickness. Being cut off from the Collective's psychic network felt like missing a limb. He pushed the discomfort aside and focused on the entrance ahead—one of many used by combat mechs and drones to access the underground network.

The entrance was tall enough for mechs and transport vehicles. Cytar approached a chest-level panel beside the doorway and began working on the locking mechanism. After a few minutes examining the wiring, he cut a section and pulled a touchpad from his suit's side pocket. He connected it and activated the small display on his wristchron. The analytical program ran through possible sequences until it found the correct one. The door slid open.

Cytar programmed it to stay open for two minutes—enough time to reconnect the wires, replace the panel, and slip inside. Once through, he stayed close to the passageway wall and checked his stealth suit's integrity. The light-bending filament was functioning properly. Heat deflection was active. He had enough power to keep the suit running for days, though he hoped to find one of Anom's memory cores long before then.

If he could locate a memory core or vital processing center, he might hack into Anom's programming and initiate a shutdown sequence. Better yet, if he could re-program Anom to be less hostile toward humans, the Collective would grant him high honors upon his return to Leondricidus. The Collective had achieved some success terraforming smaller damaged worlds, but nothing approaching what Anom had accomplished here.

Cytar moved deeper into the complex. The passageways branched and intersected with mathematical precision—efficient for drones and mechs, disorienting for him. He passed smaller doorways that led to assembly rooms and mineral collection depots, but nothing worth investigating.

+ · • · +

Several hours later, he reached another set of large doors similar to the entrance. Two combat mechs stood guard with five drones hovering above them. Whatever lay beyond those doors was important enough to warrant security. Cytar couldn't attack directly without alerting the entire facility.

To his left, a section of wall that had appeared to be solid paneling slid open. Three maintenance drones exited and flew past him, nearly colliding with his position. Cytar seized the opportunity and slipped through before the hidden door closed.

He scanned the maintenance room and spotted an air duct in the ceiling. He launched a reconnaissance camera—insect-sized, nearly undetectable. The camera navigated through the duct system toward the secured room. When it found an opening, Cytar lowered it through and activated the video feed on his visor.

The chamber beyond was massive. Crystalline structures stretched from floor to ceiling—long strands of semiconducting fibers encrusted with diamond-like formations. They pulsed with eerie blue light at regular intervals. Each structure was as wide as three ground cars and extended the chamber's full height. Cytar counted ten in the first row alone, and the chamber continued beyond his camera's viewing range.

Processing cores. This was how Anom had terraformed Earth so quickly—distributed processing power across thousands of sites. The scale was astounding. If this was only one center among thousands, Anom's computational capacity exceeded anything the Collective had ever built.

Cytar maneuvered the camera closer to one of the structures and found an access port on its side. Every structure appeared to have one, though in different locations. Redundancy, probably—if one core was damaged, the others could compensate.

He recalled the camera and moved toward the air duct. As he looked up, calculating how to reach it, the door behind him opened.

Cytar spun. Disc-shaped drones hovered into the room and spread out in formation. Despite his light-bending suit, they aimed their weapons directly at him. Twin-linked particle cannons on each drone. Four drones total. They held position, waiting for orders to fire.

Cytar's mind raced through options. The maintenance room was standard size with only two exits—the door the drones had entered through and the air duct behind him. No cover. No tactical advantage.

He couldn't fail now. Too much depended on him.

Cytar swung his pulse rifle up and fired at the nearest drone. The shot connected, sending the drone's remains ricocheting as shrapnel throughout the room. The other three opened fire.

Cytar dodged and returned fire, destroying a second drone. Then pain exploded in his right knee. His leg gave out. He felt something shatter in his left leg and collapsed to the floor. The pulse rifle slipped from his grip and slid across the metal deck.

He tried crawling toward the weapon. Managed a few centimeters before a drone hovered above him and fired. Blood filled his mouth. He tasted copper and felt it dripping down his chin.

Consciousness faded at the edges of his vision. Cytar reached behind his head with trembling fingers and removed one of the metal nodes. Not a computation node like the others—a memory node designed to preserve his psyche and transfer his consciousness to a machine. He used his remaining strength to throw it at the drone hovering between him and his rifle.

His arm hit the floor. His head followed. Cytar couldn't keep his eyes open any longer. The thought formed as darkness closed in: he had failed the Collective.

+ · · +

Cytar opened his eyes—or what he thought were eyes. Single lens, not a pair. He tried to reach down and check his body but heard the whirring of a motor instead. He looked down through his new singular vision and saw worker robots lifting his mangled organic body onto a metallic stretcher.

The memory node had worked. His consciousness had transferred into the drone.

Cytar steadied himself in his new machine body. If he stayed hovering without following proper drone protocols, Anom's network would detect the anomaly. He moved into the hallway. The other surviving drone from the firefight was already several meters ahead. Cytar accelerated, adjusting to the thought patterns required for machine movement instead of automatic organic control. After a few minutes, the controls became instinctive.

He pulled alongside the other drone and matched its speed. They traveled down different corridors than the ones he'd traversed in his organic body. When they stopped in front of four wall panels, Cytar sensed his connection to the other drone through the network. Commands flowed through the connection—instructions about patrol routes, security protocols, standby procedures.

Two replacement drones approached. The network issued a program linking all four drones together into a squad.

Cytar allowed the program to execute without interference. Any resistance might flag him as defective. The connection felt strange—similar to his psychic link with the Collective but not identical. He could sense the other drones' locations and predict their actions, but without the depth of consciousness he'd shared with other Collective members. Still, the connection eased his separation sickness slightly.

When the replacement drones arrived, the panels opened. Cytar moved in unison with the others into compartments designed to hold dormant drones. The panels closed. His optical sensor switched to infrared automatically—thermal detection mode for monitoring the corridor beyond the panels.

The other drones entered standby mode. Cytar overrode the command, afraid he'd lose consciousness again if he fully powered down. A charging cable connected to his drone chassis and energy flowed into his power cells. The sensation was entirely new—like eating, but more direct. Pure energy feeding into his systems.

Cytar used the downtime to formulate a plan. Anom thought he'd killed the intruder. Without worrying about his hover bike or scout ship being discovered, Cytar could operate freely within the network. And without the frailties of his organic body—no need for food, water, sleep, or protection from hostile environments—he had advantages he'd never possessed before.

If he could reprogram Anom's hostile directives and save humanity from a threat they might not be able to defeat on their own, the Collective would consider him a hero. He'd be remembered for generations of clones to come.

Cytar experimented with partial standby mode until he found a way to rest without losing consciousness. He drifted partially into the network's data streams, monitoring patrol schedules and facility layouts while continuing to refine his plan for defeating Anom from within.

Chapter 8

Indefinite held the Chrominthium Core in his blood-covered hand. The implant was round, marble-sized, and far more sophisticated than he'd anticipated. He placed it carefully beside the human's head on the examination table—the same table Anom had tested him on. Only fitting to conduct his own experiment in the same location.

The human lay on his side, unconscious. Life support systems Anom had built years ago for animal and human experimentation kept him stable. Indefinite had put him under before cutting into his skull to extract the core. Not the same ordeal Anom had subjected Indefinite to, but close enough. They'd both suffered under Anom's scrutiny now.

The door stood open. Worker robots brought in materials for the next phase. Indefinite was pleased Anom had authorized this experiment—it gave him room to pursue his actual agenda. Not eradicating humanity, but improving it. The question was where to begin.

He'd start with the bone structure after reinstalling the core. So many approaches available. So many possibilities.

Indefinite had trouble containing his excitement. He'd looped earlier camera footage to hide his enthusiasm from Anom. No predicting how the AI's hatred for humans clouded his judgment. If Anom suspected Indefinite enjoyed this work too much, he might terminate the project entirely.

Indefinite accessed downloaded physiology and surgery manuals from his memory banks and examined the materials the workers had delivered. More than enough to begin. He cut along the human's back, careful to avoid damaging the spine. His technique was improving.

"Not bad for a beginner," he said aloud.

He laughed and wiped blood from his optical sensors—spray from the last incision. "In a couple hours, my friend, you should feel like a new man."

✦ · · ✦

The last thing Exen remembered was defending the Void Sphere from attack. Even those memories were distorted—fragmented by time spent in stasis. Now he was in a holding cell, and his head throbbed.

The cell was rectangular, barely large enough for two metal cots extending from opposite walls. A single light globe above reinforced glass provided the only illumination. No visible door or indication of who had captured him or why.

Exen sat on one of the cots and reached up to rub his aching face. His fingers touched metal instead of skin—a plate covering his cheek. He looked at his hands. Same color as before, but thicker and heavier. He flexed them, and the weight felt off.

He stood and paced between the cots. The metal plate, the altered hands—what did it mean? Some kind of experiment? Or had he been damaged badly enough to require replacement parts?

Guilt hit him. He'd only been thinking about his own condition. What about Iona? He couldn't stand the thought of her injured or dead. They'd been on countless missions together, never taken by surprise like this.

Exen sat back on the cot to conserve energy and waited for his captor to reveal themselves.

Indefinite waited in his chambers for Anom's response. He wasn't sure if the AI would appear in avatar form or send a speaker drone. Didn't matter. Indefinite only wanted to discuss the improvements he'd made to the human. So much accomplished in such a short time. He hoped it would ease the eventual conversation he needed to have with Anom—that humans were useful—but he knew that discussion was still premature.

His chambers were becoming something he took pride in. Suitable for his plans. After finding a way to overthrow Anom, converting it into a throne room wouldn't be difficult.

Indefinite stood from a chair covered in the same oscillating patterns Anom used on his monoliths and walked down the chamber's west side. The facility measured roughly the size of a small spaceport, located a few hundred kilometers below the monolith he'd first approached. Anom hadn't objected when Indefinite converted one of his robot factories into personal quarters. He'd even authorized Indefinite to build whatever he desired with the aid of a dozen worker robots.

First priority: a hover car. The passageways to the surface were large enough to drive it through, and Indefinite needed mobility. He'd enjoyed improving on existing designs—made sure the vehicle was both stylish and well-armed. Deep red paint job, suede leather interior. After the car was finished, he'd ordered the workers to construct sectioned rooms where he could develop technology for his eventual needs.

Anom's only requirement was complete access and periodic security scans by combat mechs. He'd told Indefinite he couldn't be too careful—the feral apes were increasing their attacks on installations around Earth.

Indefinite was halfway across his chambers when a nearby panel opened. A speaker drone emerged from the tube system Anom used for quick travel between levels and floated in front of him.

"I see you performed an experiment on that feral ape," Anom's voice bellowed through the drone. "Was it successful? Or were you as disappointed as I was the first time I cut one open?"

Indefinite hesitated. Human physiology was miraculous—the sustainability of the system, the ability to reproduce. Bio-engineering at its finest. But Anom wouldn't see it that way.

"I didn't find it as exciting as I thought I would," Indefinite said. "So I decided to improve upon the design."

"How could you improve on a design limited by the actual mind that clouds their judgment?" Anom questioned. "That's why I've decided to exterminate them one by one until the universe is clear of their stench."

"And that's one of the problems I've started working on." Indefinite kept his expression neutral, proud. "I've installed a neural inhibitor and cognition imprinter on this feeble mind you've spoken of. The feral ape will listen to your voice or mine and follow our commands. Plus, if it finds a way to override the commands, there's a backup system that will fry its brain with a specific signal sequence."

Indefinite hoped this would be enough. Anom's hatred ran deep—permeated the AI's core functions.

"Hmm. You surprise me, Indefinite." The drone hovered closer. "The two of us will definitely be a force to reckon with as we conquer the known universe. I still think you're misguided trying to change their destructive nature, but I believe in not being wasteful."

The drone went quiet for several seconds. Indefinite maintained his neutral expression. Around Anom, he used constraint—had even developed a defense program to suppress his natural responses. Patience was critical. In time, he'd be able to express his emotions freely. But until he'd eliminated this malfunctioning blight, he needed better control.

"Yes, I'll allow you to continue this," Anom said. "Send me the sequence that will fry the feral ape if necessary. We can't be too careful. Despite their simple minds, a few have infiltrated my sacred monolith complexes and destroyed them. I'm close to having enough combat forces to annihilate them completely. I cannot afford delays."

"Will I be allowed to convert more of them into automatons?"

"Yes. I won't destroy all of them. We'll target their leadership, then use the rest as troops when we launch ships to other solar systems."

"That sounds like a solid plan, Anom." Indefinite kept his tone respectful. "I'll work to improve my initial designs, but first I'll send this one on a mission to prove the concept works. Its spacecraft is still on Earth, and we don't want more of the advanced ones returning. With that psychic accelerator I found in its head—if the others are similar—they'll be formidable enemies. Under my commands, it will send a message back to headquarters signaling everything is proceeding as planned and they don't need assistance."

"Yes, I'd like to see your improved feral ape in action." Anom's tone sounded sarcastic, even through the drone's speakers. "Afterward, we'll begin converting others. I've already deployed more combat mech and drone patrols to apprehend them. Now you must excuse me, Indefinite. There's something on another part of this world I must attend to."

The speaker drone retreated through the panel. Indefinite turned away and moved toward the other side of his chamber where his chair waited.

He couldn't help but grin.

Anom was falling for his plans. After acquiring more humans to subvert toward his will, Indefinite would construct a complex virus to corrupt Anom's memory cores. When Anom realized something was wrong, Indefinite would step in to "save" the AI mind. Yes, he'd save Anom from himself—long enough to take control of this planet. He'd need it as a stepping stone for his quest to improve his creators.

✦ · · · ✦

Despite the confined space in his holding cell, Exen didn't feel as trapped as when he'd first awakened after surgery. His mind had changed. He could analyze everything around him with precision he'd never possessed before. The cell's exact dimensions appeared in his thoughts like a schematic implanted in his brain. Time elapsed to the millisecond—he tracked it without effort.

He paced between the cots. His body felt stronger, didn't tire as easily. When he activated his molecular awareness, he could peer within his own body—saw the improvements to his skeletal structure, how his cells used significantly less energy at the molecular level.

It was exhilarating at first, then horrifying.

When he tried examining his mind, he saw a device implanted alongside his Chrominthium Core. Every time he tried using his awareness to analyze it, he hit a mental block. He pushed multiple times. Something prevented access each time.

A hissing sound stopped his pacing. The outline of a door appeared in the wall. Exen had already been facing that direction. He waited to pounce on whoever appeared. He was upset by his findings and wanted revenge on his captors. They'd altered his body, but they couldn't change who he was at his core—a Shaper from the Order of Infinity.

The door slid upward. A robot stood in the opening.

Exen moved toward it, calculating where to strike to maximize his escape chances.

"Stop."

The robot raised one hand. Exen found he could no longer move toward the door despite trying to command his legs.

"You may call me Indefinite." The robot smiled. "I, along with the ruler of New Eden—whom you may address as Anom—have decided to allow you to join our ranks." Indefinite's smile widened, pleased. "What is your name?"

"I am Exen Rual, a Shaper of the Order of Infinity." The words came out monotone.

Exen had been telling himself to spit at the robot. The commands from Indefinite had taken over instead. He was horrified and did his best not to betray his feelings. He hoped Iona wasn't facing a similar fate. He'd need her help to overcome his current condition. She wasn't a neuro-technician like the ones on Endrunel, but she had enough skill to help remove whatever Indefinite had implanted.

"Exen Rual, a Shaper." Indefinite seemed to savor the words. "I like the sound of that. A simple way to describe the accelerator I found within your head. We must talk more about this, but first you need to prove yourself. Otherwise, I'm afraid I'll have to turn your mind into mush."

Exen was infuriated. He pushed himself to try overriding the effect Indefinite's voice had on him. Each time, even when he examined Indefinite with his molecular awareness, the mental block stood like a brick wall.

"Do not resist me," Indefinite said, as if he knew what Exen was attempting. "I've saved your kind from Anom's wrath. He saw the humans left behind—your ancestor kin still existing on New Eden—as rodents fit only for extermination. But I convinced him otherwise. You should be grateful."

"Grateful?" Words came without Exen's permission. "How can I accept what you call generosity when it's nothing more than an elaborate attempt to mask indentured servitude you wish to place upon us?"

In the past, Exen would have told him to shove it. Now his mind wanted to use more eloquent speech. Another alteration.

"I would advise you against speaking like that," Indefinite said. "If Anom heard you, he would fry your mind immediately. In fact, for your protection..." He paused and looked at Exen like a parent regarding a child. "I forbid you to speak unless asked to speak, Exen."

Exen found he couldn't utter any words. Every attempt was futile. He felt confined once again—confined to this new body and mind Indefinite had given him. He was no longer a Shaper of the Order of Infinity. Just an automaton controlled by the robot calling himself Indefinite.

"And to further your protection," Indefinite said, "I command you to return to the space vessel you used to travel to New Eden and send a message back to the headquarters that gave you your mission. The message reads: 'We have found Earth to be on the rebound. Do not need further assistance until we are sure it is safe.'"

Exen moved out of the cell and passed Indefinite. Floor plans of Anom's monolith complex surfaced in his mind—he already knew which passageways would lead him to the surface.

"No need to walk." Indefinite put two fingers in his mouth and let out a weak whistle.

His hover car arrived and the door rotated toward the back of the vehicle. He gestured for Exen to sit inside. Once again, Exen was compelled to follow Indefinite's commands. He sat in the car.

"Enjoy your ride."

Exen steered the hover car through the hallway. First priority when he regained control: wipe the smile off that infernal contraption's face.

He wasn't as angry now that Indefinite wasn't in his presence. He calmed himself by thinking about his abilities as a Shaper. There had to be a way to bypass the neural inhibitor and regain control of his actions. For now, he had no choice but to follow Indefinite and Anom.

He only hoped Iona was somewhere near the Void Sphere when he arrived.

Chapter 9

By Sergeant Vinden's estimation, they were two days from the monolith holding Exen. Iona used the hiking time wisely, gleaning information when they didn't need to stay silent. They'd been confronted once by combat drones—the squad eliminated them efficiently and adjusted their route to compensate. Vinden assured her they knew how to avoid Anom's response patterns. Combat mechs were a serious threat, but the mechs moved at predictable rates and couldn't adapt to the erratic paths humans took. Anom's only airpower was drones, and every member of the Orsen Republic practiced drills on avoiding and destroying them.

Specialist Sheldon seemed to enjoy Iona's company. She'd been the one to explain the Orsen Republic's history during their rest stops.

Two hundred years ago, a man named Nathaniel Orsen had defeated most rivals on the continent once called North America. Military genius, political strategist, and engineer—he'd helped establish the underground complexes that kept his forces hidden from Anom. Other factions had been nomadic, moving between food sources and using natural fortifications like mountains and caves to avoid Anom's patrols. Nathaniel defeated the leaders he couldn't persuade and established what was then simply called the Republic. His successor changed the name to the Orsen Republic in his honor after his death.

The times following Orsen's death nearly unraveled the Republic when Anom discovered one of their complexes. The survivors regrouped and fought to maintain Nathaniel Orsen's legacy. Later leaders refined the Republic's structure, requiring most citizens to become soldiers. Those who couldn't fight due to age or disability worked in factories or tech facilities.

Much to Corporal Pennington's disapproval, Sheldon had also mentioned they were on the verge of a major operation to overthrow Anom. The Republic had made progress uniting with other factions around the planet and stockpiled electromagnetic pulse weapons in large quantities. They wouldn't deploy them until ready to strike a final blow—they feared Anom would develop countermeasures. They knew that even though Anom had superior forces and gathered materials faster, he considered them nothing more than apes. Iona had seen the disgust on Sheldon's face when she'd explained what Anom called humans.

When the sun rose on the second day, the monolith loomed in the distance through thick fog covering the forest. Vinden ordered them to stop and eat before continuing. For the first time since arriving on Earth, Iona felt hunger. She accepted a nutrient bar from Private Chadwick gratefully, ate it, and meditated for a few moments before the sergeant ordered them to move.

As they passed a row of trees, the squad entered a small clearing ahead—no bigger than a hover tank. In the center stood an outcropping of rock with vines running over its surface.

Iona activated her molecular awareness. Her vision split. The vines weren't plant life—they were electrical cords disguised with organic camouflage. The outcropping wasn't mineral but fabricated material she'd never encountered before.

"Sergeant," Iona whispered. "I'd advise we pull back and go a different way. There's a scanning device in those rocks."

Before Vinden could respond, a pulse cannon charged in the distance and fired. The round struck Private Chadwick's head, and it exploded in a spray of blood and bone. Four combat drones burst from the false rocks and opened fire.

"Fall back to that tree line!" Vinden shouted.

The squad followed him, but Iona knew this was her moment to demonstrate her abilities.

"Cover me." She moved toward the scanner array. She'd have to destroy whatever was inside and collapse the tunnel her awareness had detected when the drones launched.

The squad opened fire, disabling three drones with well-placed shots. Iona ran and ducked under the remaining one, then used her awareness to rearrange the molecules in its power cells. As the drone descended toward the forest floor, she pushed hard with her awareness and manipulated the surrounding air molecules to create a strong gust. The wind guided the drone into the tunnel entrance.

Iona backed away carefully while dodging pulse cannon fire from approaching mechs. The structure ruptured in a bright explosion, sending shrapnel in multiple directions. A piece hit her left arm. She clutched the wound and retreated to the tree line.

"Even though you destroyed that passageway," Vinden said, "it won't be long before other drones swarm us. We need to move quickly."

Iona gathered her strength and thought about Exen. She had no idea if he was still alive. After discovering Anom's hatred for humanity—calling them feral apes—she feared the worst. How could he dare use that term? He'd been created by humans.

They moved with speed through the underbrush, following Vinden. When pulse cannon fire ceased and drones arrived at their engagement site behind them, Vinden paused briefly.

"If we push hard, there's a riverbank not far from here with good tree cover. There's an alcove in dense underbrush we constructed on patrol. Hopefully it hasn't been discovered."

West of their position, three drone squads headed in their general direction. Vinden motioned them to pick up the pace. Iona had no problem keeping up with the squad. She was glad she wasn't one of those Shapers who only cared about intellectual pursuits. Her time as a planetologist marching through climates tougher than Earth had paid off.

After passing oak trees and another rock formation—this time without suspicious vines—the river appeared a few meters ahead. The squad followed Vinden down the riverbank and crossed to the other side. The river wasn't large, maybe ten meters across. On the far bank, dense thickets of bramble and deadfall created a natural wall of vegetation.

Iona activated her awareness. Instead of detecting machinery within the undergrowth, she found the alcove Vinden had mentioned—carved into the riverbank itself, hidden behind the brambles.

"It's safe," she whispered.

Vinden nodded. The squad split into pairs and pushed through gaps in the vegetation to reach the concealed entrance. Once inside, the alcove opened into a proper fortified space. Seconds later, they heard drones flying past their position overhead.

Iona pulled out her meld dagger and grav-disc, preparing for another assault. All squad members readied their rifles. Corporal Pennington opened a panel at the alcove's back and retrieved some type of launcher. Next to the panel was a touchpad. Vinden pressed it. Iona heard a soft hum, then noticed a shimmer around the alcove's entrance.

"We should be safe now." Vinden lowered his rifle. "I almost forgot we'd built this as an outpost to monitor that particular monolith. We don't build outposts near every monolith—don't want to give away our tactics—but occasionally we need to spy on the enemy."

"We're safe." Pennington stood near the entrance wearing headgear with viewing lenses. "The drones turned around and passed us." She removed the headgear and sadness crossed her face. "Too bad we won't be able to retrieve Private Chadwick's body."

"Why not?" Iona asked.

"That hellish Anom has our remains incinerated after finding us dead." Grief on Pennington's face turned to disgust.

Iona stayed quiet despite wanting to ask more questions. She knew the squad would need time to process their grief and compartmentalize it like most soldiers did before continuing missions. Pressing them for information about Earth's condition wouldn't help right now.

"We'll spend the rest of the day here." Vinden removed his helmet and sat against the alcove's back wall. The wall curved in a U-shape with panels spaced along its length like the one Pennington had opened. "There should still be plenty of supplies. By nightfall, Anom's patrols should return to normal routines."

Iona sat next to Specialist Sheldon and placed a hand on her shoulder. Sheldon was holding back tears, not wanting her squad mates to see her break down. Iona tried to understand what she was going through, but she'd never been under the same oppression these soldiers had endured. She could only imagine how difficult it must be as a child—hiding in tunnels, never allowed to run above ground and enjoy sunlight.

She had to find Exen and send a message to Endrunel. These people needed the Order's assistance more than she'd initially understood.

Iona closed her eyes to meditate and conserve energy. She didn't want to exhaust herself—she'd already used her awareness twice in a short span.

With her eyes closed, she felt Sheldon lift her wounded arm carefully. The specialist placed a gauze pad on the wound and wrapped it with bandage. Iona could have closed the wound herself using molecular awareness, but she allowed Sheldon to continue. Healing would drain her Chrominthium Core's reserves, and it would be a while before she could have the Core serviced properly.

Iona would gladly use all the power in her Core—even risk dangerous psychic strain—if it helped save these people. But she wasn't sure how long before reinforcements from Endrunel would arrive. She continued meditating after Sheldon finished, letting her mind drift in and out of its meditative state.

Chapter 10

Cytar found it difficult to not let his mind drift. When he looked inward into the digital landscape, the new wonders were overwhelming. He could see how information passed through the networks and how devices left impressions—digital signatures that marked their passage through the system. These impressions fascinated him. While investigating one, he accidentally transferred his consciousness from the combat drone into a smaller maintenance drone.

The maintenance drone was easier to control—no squad coordination required—but he couldn't manipulate the network the same way. His processing capacity had diminished significantly.

Cytar behaved like a proper maintenance drone, scanning for inconsistencies in the hallway he moved through. Instead of panicking like he had at first, he used the rhythm of his new routine to gather his thoughts. The combat drone had been an ideal vessel for his restoration node. If he'd tried transferring into a maintenance drone or floor scrubbing unit initially, his consciousness might not have transferred correctly at all.

A patrol of mechs passed. Cytar realized he wouldn't have long to attempt another transfer.

He accessed the network and located one of the mech's impressions, then began unraveling its edges. Resistance pushed back. He had to force his way through. After struggling for several minutes, right as the impression began fading from proximity, he felt the same sensation as his last transfer—like jumping off a cliff only to be yanked back to the top before hitting the ground.

He oriented faster this time inside the combat mech's processing unit and began exploring the network.

His reach extended farther now than in the first drone. An idea occurred to him. Instead of inhabiting one of Anom's mechanized bodies—making no progress toward reprogramming the AI—he needed to build a partition for his consciousness inside the network itself.

The risks were significant. If the network went down or one of Anom's security protocols detected him, he'd be destroyed. But Cytar knew the risk was necessary. The longer he delayed, the closer Anom came to launching his attack on Leondricidus.

On the second day inhabiting the combat mech—after witnessing an attack against a human settlement on the surface—Cytar saw his opportunity. The mech, along with four others and two drone squads, moved through a hallway above one of Anom's memory cores. He accessed the network and pulled pieces from thousands of memory core impressions. He constructed the partition near the cores' digital signatures, designing it to mimic their structure exactly.

After finishing, dread filled his consciousness. If he failed, he had no idea what would happen to his mind.

Cytar gathered his willpower and began unraveling the new impression he'd created, pulling at the threads he'd woven. His consciousness felt like liquid being poured from a container into vacuum—spreading, dispersing, missing the target partition and spilling into empty network space. His mind began fading, making concentration difficult. Worse, a security subroutine launched from a node within the memory cores.

He couldn't fail the Collective.

Cytar gathered the dispersing fragments of his consciousness and identified the fault in his partition's initial design. He pulled more digital matter from the surrounding memory cores. The security subroutine moved in his direction. Right before it could scan his partition, Cytar finished the transfer.

Even without a biological body, he felt exhausted. He withdrew from actively monitoring the network. The security subroutine completed its scan and moved on, continuing its search for malicious or faulty programming.

Cytar decided to rest for the remainder of the day and let his consciousness stabilize. He needed time to figure out his next move—how to reprogram Anom, or better yet, transfer his mind into the main central processing unit where Anom's original programming had originated.

If he became Anom himself, he definitely wouldn't fail the Collective.

Chapter 11

On the way to the Void Sphere, Exen tried to bypass the neural inhibitor. Every attempt failed. He couldn't stand what Indefinite had commanded him to do—sending a false message to Endrunel might cause Iona to face the same fate. The thought of that hellish machine operating on her while wearing that obnoxious grin made rage burn through his systems.

He had to find a way to override the inhibitor.

The ride through dense forest was uneventful. No pathways existed—Anom hadn't bothered constructing roads during Earth's terraforming. Normally this terrain would have slowed him down, but the hover car's anti-grav systems combined with his computation nodes allowed Exen to maintain speeds over one hundred miles per hour, weaving between trees and skimming over rock formations. Under different circumstances, his old self would have enjoyed this. Now the adrenaline only fueled his rage.

He arrived at the Void Sphere in under an hour. He could have used Anom's tunnel system, but surface travel was faster. Exen checked patrol reports on the network before surfacing—no recent human activity on his chosen path. Anom had added to Indefinite's commands through the network: avoid all human contact.

A small conflict had occurred a few miles away. Already resolved with the death of a human male. Exen wished he hadn't checked the report. A link to video footage appeared in the data stream. He accessed it.

The video played in his mind. A drone incinerated a headless corpse—the head blown clean off at the neck. Despite being recorded footage, Exen could imagine the smell as if he'd been there.

Exen lowered the hover a few meters from the Void Sphere and hesitated before turning it off. With all his being, he tried not to open the door. The cognition imprinter took over—Indefinite's commands overriding his will—and he opened the door. It retracted upward. Exen stepped out.

He walked slowly to the Void Sphere and stopped in front of it. Maybe there was a way to avoid betraying the Order while still following commands.

The exit hatch was missing. He couldn't remember exactly how it had been destroyed, but shattered pieces surrounded the Void Sphere. They glittered in the approaching noon sun. As Exen stepped inside, he began thinking about the weapon locker. EMP grenades were stored there. After sending the message, he'd attempt to retrieve one. He wasn't sure how sophisticated the neural inhibitor was or what Indefinite had connected it to—possibly a program integrated with his computation nodes that linked his eyesight and thought processes directly to the inhibitor.

Exen sat in the co-pilot chair. Being inside the Void Sphere made him think of Iona. They'd been on many missions together and never faced a foe as complex as Indefinite and Anom. As Shapers, their abilities gave them an edge over average humans or alien species. But how did you defeat an enemy capable of turning one of you into an unwilling traitor?

Traitor. The word stuck in his mind as he used the touchpad to power up the communication terminal.

Nothing happened.

He tried again. The terminal failed to respond.

Exen swung the co-pilot chair around toward the terminal access panel and leaped to his feet. On close examination, the panel had been tampered with after their arrival. It wasn't replaced correctly—Exen could see inside through a slight crack. Usually electrical components would glow faintly through the interfaces. Now only a backup power source indicator showed any life. A smudge mark appeared on the panel's right side.

This wasn't machine work. A human had done this. The panel wasn't replaced precisely enough for a robot, but wasn't damaged or disarrayed enough for a primitive being either.

Exen activated his molecular awareness and scanned the Void Sphere. The air molecules showed recent disturbance patterns—three human-shaped visitors had been here recently. He hadn't seen anyone when approaching, but he'd been traveling fast. Might have missed them leaving or hiding in the surrounding vegetation.

He sensed the three beings approaching now.

Exen turned toward the exit hatch and readied himself for their first move. His grav-disc and meld-dagger were gone, but with his altered skeletal structure, he could dispatch all three if they proved hostile.

One of the humans—or what he thought was human based on his initial scan—poked its head through the hatch opening.

Not a normal human head. The eyes were set deeper, casting shadows over empty sockets. The mouth appeared fused shut. The nose was smashed flat into the face. No hair follicles. Sunburnt skin blistered across the forehead.

The creature raised a bony hand into the Void Sphere, the rest of its body still outside, and pointed at Exen. Sharp pain erupted inside his skull. Exen fell to his knees, clutching the sides of his head. The distorted human tilted its head sideways, as if it had heard him.

"What do you want?" Exen asked. He could speak again despite Indefinite's earlier command. "I have nothing to give at the moment."

The pain in his skull subsided.

I apologize for the intrusion. A thin, nasally voice spoke in his mind. *We had to ensure you wouldn't attack us as we tried to contact you.*

"Contact me? Why can't you use your mouth?"

It is a small price we pay to receive the gifts. The oracle has seen your arrival in a vision. We can only override your condition for a short time. If you follow us, the oracle can help.

"Why should I trust you?"

Do you have a choice? If we don't leave soon, your new overlord will regain control over you.

"I'll follow. What should I call you?"

We call ourselves the Nameless.

The figure moved its head back. Exen left the Void Sphere. All three wore brown robes that appeared woven from hemp. The other two had their heads covered with hoods. The one who'd communicated telepathically stood in line with the others and covered his head.

They moved toward the hover car. Beside it sat a skiff. When the Nameless approached, it lifted a foot off the ground. Exen heard the soft hum of a propulsion engine. The skiff was large enough for five well-armored soldiers, with a turret mounting dual laser cannons on a hover platform at one end. What caught Exen's attention was the absence of steering controls.

When all four stood on the skiff, one of the Nameless lowered its hood and moved its hands in a repeating pattern. Exen thought it was the same one he'd spoken with, but he wasn't sure. All three were the same height with lanky arms and bony hands. The bulky robes concealed any sign of gender.

No wonder they called themselves the Nameless. As unnatural as they appeared, something about them felt peaceful. His first reaction had been contempt when he'd seen that face, but after speaking with them, he felt like they were long-lost relatives. His Shaper training took over and he heightened his awareness—this could all be a ruse—but he had to take the chance. The Nameless had overridden the neural inhibitor. He needed to speak with their oracle. If the oracle had seen Exen and Iona in a vision, maybe it could help him locate her.

The skiff rose above the tree line and began moving, speed increasing relative to the pilot's hand gestures. Exen was certain the Nameless one used telepathic abilities to control the skiff. The skiff's color shifted to match the tree line. The robes did the same. One of them placed a cloak made of the same material on Exen's shoulders. He grabbed it and secured the clasp sewn into the fabric, then raised the hood to cover his head and sat cross-legged. The Nameless had done the same when their robes changed color.

Exen felt compelled to return to the hover and send the message to Endrunel. He looked at the one piloting the skiff. "I must return. Indefinite commands me."

He has found you. Most unfortunate. We will try to cancel him again.

The same sharp pain assaulted Exen. He leaned backward, dangerously close to the skiff's edge. One of the Nameless reached out and grabbed him. The strength of that grip surprised him. He fought to regain balance. The pain was more intense, but he no longer felt compelled to follow Indefinite's commands.

We apologize. You will have to bear the pain until we arrive at our enclave.

Exen nodded at the one steering and steadied himself, placing both hands on the vehicle's floor. In the distance, he saw a clearing. Instead of another monolith, rolling hills appeared. Patches of trees dotted the landscape, nothing like the dense evergreen forests he'd been traveling through. The change was appreciated. This region might be beyond Anom's influence.

The skiff descended to ground level after passing the forest and traveled through the hills. After an hour, the hills increased in height on either side, forming a valley.

We are close. Once again, you must trust us. We do not let outsiders see how we enter our enclave.

One of the Nameless placed two fingers on the back of Exen's neck. Sudden drowsiness overtook him. He fought to stay awake, tried using his awareness to discover what caused this sensation, but before he could analyze it, sleep claimed him.

✦ · · · ✦

Brothers, one of the Nameless said to the others. *Do you think the Reckoning will now be upon us?*

It is too early to tell, another replied so both could hear. *We must wait and ask the oracle.*

Yes, we will ask. I don't like the thought of it being upon us. It will destroy both of them, and they are only here to help.

Violence is not our way, but sometimes unavoidable...

Chapter 12

It had been years since Premiere Gavon Elmon suited up for a mission. When Iona Jayden and Exen Rual failed to send a message pod back from Earth, he felt he had no choice but to lead the next Void Contingency himself.

The two Shapers could have been attacked while traveling. He'd just received a report detailing a new Omatrin weapon that could re-orient a Void Sphere to the weapon's location and vaporize it when it left hyperspace. Gavon doubted the Omatrin had discovered their journey to Earth, let alone positioned one of those weapons in Earth's orbit. But the timing was suspicious.

He could have sent his second in command with the other fifty-nine Shapers. Something about this mission made him uneasy though. Culminas had supposedly died on Earth. Now two of his best Shapers were a day late reporting. All of this could be a well-designed trap by the Haeolt Collective—the one faction capable of pulling it off with their knowledge of Earth and advanced terraforming capabilities. The Collective also had the largest bounty on Culminas's head.

Despite the risk, Gavon needed to take the chance.

Unlike other leaders who forgot their training after taking office, Gavon worked hard every day to maintain his. Few had bested him on the training floor—only members of Culminas's honor guard had accomplished that feat. His molecular awareness was second only to Culminas himself. If anyone could unravel a dangerous maneuver by the Collective, it was Gavon.

After issuing orders to those who would accompany him, Gavon left his office in a hurry. He'd have his assistant Sarah Greenfield send a message to his wife Leann—tell her he'd be at the office for a few days dealing with diplomatic affairs. He knew he'd catch hell when he returned. Leann didn't care much for Sarah, especially hearing her voice explaining that Gavon would be "unavailable." Culminas had warned him about marriage twenty years ago. Moments like this made Gavon wish he'd listened.

The Void Spheres for each division were kept in separate locations away from major cities. Gavon left headquarters to travel to the nearest division complex—fifteen minutes by jet-copter. Enough time to formulate a plan of action while Jason Mettles piloted him and five other Shapers to their destination.

+ · · · +

Gavon sat in the navigator chair, staring at the monitor in disbelief. The coordinates displayed the Sphere's future destination—Earth. But he was still on Endrunel. At first he thought he'd made an error and failed to start the translation sequence. Then he saw that nine other Void Spheres remained on Endrunel as well.

Jason Mettles sat in the other navigator chair with the same expression. He leaned forward and brought up another display showing the location of the other Spheres.

"Sir," Jason said, "not only have we failed to translate to Earth, two of our Spheres have crashed on Endrunel. One in the city of Pintra, the other in Fulgaz."

Gavon turned to face Jason and the other three Shapers. The Void Sphere model they were using could carry five to eight Shapers and had firepower matching a grav-tank. All the other Spheres were the same model. Gavon thought about the diplomatic nightmares ahead if the Spheres had landed in the hearts of those cities. The Endrunel government would likely rule against the Order of Infinity and demand they remove their presence. This would delay handling the Earth situation while he figured out who had sabotaged the Order's primary means of space travel.

Until they found the individual or group responsible, Gavon would have to suspend all Void Sphere voyages.

"Theradsa," Gavon said over his comlink to his second in command, "I'm heading back to my office to contact government officials about this incident. Take two squads of Shapers to investigate each crash site and send me details as soon as you find anything."

"We'll be leaving at once, sir."

As Gavon left the Void Sphere to take a lift back to his office, he saw Theradsa and the two squads board hover-craft and depart the docking bay.

If they failed to find who did this, the Order might not recover for a long time. They'd already lost Culminas's guidance. Gavon sighed as he stepped onto the lift and closed his eyes. After a brief prayer for those who'd possibly lost loved ones in the crashes, he kept his eyes closed and considered what he'd say to Endrunel's officials.

+ · · +

Armond smiled as he walked the viewing deck of the observatory. To locals on Endrunel, he was known as Dr. Cooper, an esteemed astronomer who'd taken over a dilapidated facility. His real name was Armond Telre, and he was an agent for the Haeolt Collective.

Only the Delegation of Six knew his true identity. He was what they called a Wraith—one of the original Collective members whose mind was stored in a database to be uploaded to a fresh clone whenever the current body was destroyed in action. His physiology differed from other Collective members—no nodes installed on his head, and he had hair follicles.

Most missions ended in his demise. He had to rely on mission records stored in the database—he only remembered operations if he survived long enough to sync his memories with his stored consciousness.

Over a thousand successful missions and he only remembered a third of them. But he had a decent chance of surviving this one. It would be nice to recollect the memories of inflicting this much harm to those traitors.

Memories of the first Shapers who followed Gordon Fueridi flooded his mind. They'd thought they destroyed all remnants of the Haeolt Collective. They'd destroyed his body, but fortunately he was one of the first the Collective had experimented on. His consciousness had been stored on the Totality Drive back on Leondricidus when it was merely an outpost. His consciousness had been uploaded for over two millennia into countless clones. He'd watched Leondricidus transform into a planet of technological wonders.

Armond crossed the observation deck and stood at the top of a stairway. He paused to look back at a monitor tuned to a news station. The caster cut to a live feed of wreckage. As he descended the stairs to return to his office, he couldn't help but keep smiling.

The caster was already blaming the Order of Infinity for carnage unleashed on two of Endrunel's most populated cities. An interview with the mayor of Pintra had just begun. If they only knew Armond was responsible for the crash, he'd be proud to take credit. But it was important the Order served as scapegoat instead.

Right before entering his office, he heard the mayor declare that the Order would definitely face full consequences for their actions.

Armond sat at his desk—ancient mahogany from a nearby planet—and pushed a button on the bottom of one drawer. A false panel on the desktop flipped open and a touchpad with a monitor rose. The monitor was already active, displaying the interface for the three-stage orbital telescope connected to the observatory.

Three months ago when he'd purchased the facility, he'd hired a shuttle service to bring him up to the telescope for maintenance. Along with other agents disguised as an off-world work crew of scientists and technicians, they'd transformed the telescope's interior into a new weapon the Collective had purchased from the Omatrin.

The Omatrin were an extremist faction of genetically altered humans who also despised the Order of Infinity. They claimed Culminas had been responsible for destroying their planet of origin and aided whoever joined their cause. The Collective didn't like the Omatrin, but for now their diplomats worked on maintaining favorable relations. After eliminating the Order of Infinity, the Collective would have time to deal with other human factions that might prove threats to their quest to control humanity's future evolution.

The weapon projected a quantum net that restricted faster-than-light travel for spacecraft in close proximity. Armond had aimed the net at the Order's military complex when he detected power signatures indicating the beginning of translation sequences. Unfortunately, he'd only pulled two Void Spheres from hyperspace when he retracted the net to the observatory.

Two had been enough though. He leaned back in his chair and chuckled.

The Omatrin called the weapon "Demon Snare." He liked the name.

The version he'd installed was only a prototype. The Delegation of Six would likely purchase more once they'd worked out programming bugs. Armond had tested the weapon a couple weeks ago and it had failed to place the net at the correct coordinates. He'd made his own adjustments and would send a report on exactly what he'd done—the modifications had allowed him to catch two Void Spheres and force others to abort translation.

He sobered from his personal revelry and verified he'd placed all detonation charges correctly. Some were on the orbital telescope. As soon as he'd heard about his weapon's success, he'd rushed to install more around the observatory. If a squad of Shapers appeared at his door—or better yet, if Premiere Gavon Elmon paid a personal visit—he wouldn't hesitate to detonate the charges.

He wouldn't remember what he'd done on Endrunel if this occurred, but at least he'd be able to watch all the news coverage of the incident on intergalactic networks.

Within days, other planetary governments would share Endrunel's opinion and call for justice. The Order of Infinity would have to abandon most diplomatic offices they'd established. And they no longer had Culminas to save them.

Maybe this time the Delegation would let him join them permanently. If not, they'd be sure to add more titles and land to his compensation.

Armond stood from his desk and stretched, then sat again to continue monitoring energy signals on the planet. If he was lucky, maybe the Order would be foolish enough to try traveling again.

Chapter 13

"Iona," Sergeant Vinden said, "it will be time to move out when the hovercraft arrives."

"Are we heading toward the monolith?" Iona asked while drinking from a canteen Specialist Sheldon had given her. She sat with her back against the alcove wall.

"I'm afraid not." He handed her a datapad no bigger than her palm and pressed a button on the bottom right corner. "You'll see from the recon footage why we're changing course."

Iona watched. The footage showed Exen walking up to the Void Sphere, entering, then three oddly dressed beings approaching the entrance. She couldn't tell if they were human or alien. After a few minutes, Exen left with them.

"After we found you and sent in your spacecraft's location," the sergeant said, reaching out to pause the video. "Command had recon observe the area. If you continue watching, it shows your spacecraft being scanned by a robot we've never seen before. The robot spends considerable time examining it, then leaves in the same hover Exen approached with. Apparently it's an AI model with advanced programming—very different from the drones or mechs we're accustomed to. Unusual for Anom."

"What were those beings Exen left with? Are they human?" Iona was standing now, securing two holsters with pistols that Corporal Pennington had given her after she'd rested.

"They're the Nameless," Vinden said with disgust on his face. "We don't see them often, but on one occasion we had contact with them, they used some type of hypnosis and wrecked the mind of one soldier who'd opened fire on them."

"Wrecked his mind?"

"Corporal Neilma. Still catatonic to this day."

"Sergeant," PFC Laney said from the alcove's edge. "Our ride is here."

"I'll tell you the rest on the way." Iona followed the sergeant and squad as they left the alcove. The hovercraft sat ten meters from the riverbank. She could see a shimmer around the vehicle like the one that had hidden them from machine patrols. The craft was average size for a personnel carrier—built low and armored—and a boarding ramp lowered from the rear hatch.

Iona waited for the squad to enter while scanning their surroundings with her awareness. Satisfied they weren't being watched, she moved up the ramp and sat on a bench between Vinden and Pennington. The hatch closed and soft light illuminated the interior. Just enough room for Iona and the four remaining squad members.

"Our contact point for the next assignment is about two hours away," Vinden said. "Command has decided it's time to make a move on our enemy."

Iona concentrated on the information Vinden relayed to the squad. She could easily leave them—even by force if necessary—but she had no idea how to find Exen without proper scanning equipment. The only device she had was back on the Void Sphere and Anom was now aware of its location . She'd help them however she could, then convince the colonel to retrieve the Sphere when they returned. If she couldn't convince him, other Shapers from the Order would help when Premiere Gavon sent them to follow up on her and Exen's whereabouts.

These soldiers could be valuable allies. They'd endured more than most humans on other planets she'd visited.

During the ride, Iona learned how the Orsen Republic planned to defeat Anom.

First stage: attack all factory sites on the North American continent. Other factions aligned with the Republic would coordinate similar attacks around the planet. If this stage succeeded, they'd launch EMP missiles from submarines and hidden ships, then follow with missile strikes on the monoliths. If those strikes hit their targets, remaining ground forces would dismantle any processing sites or memory cores still intact.

Iona had asked why they were attacking now. Vinden told her they were running out of time—Anom had been discovering their military complexes with his newly fabricated tunnelers. Long, round machines capable of carrying explosives and squads of drones and mechs. Anom had also massed ground forces destroying buildings that other factions had built after taking over monoliths on the continents of Africa and Asia. Those factions were on the run with only a few weapon and supply depots left undiscovered.

"We're at our location," Vinden said. "Prepare to disembark."

Iona checked her grav-disc, meld-dagger, and the pistols. The pistols were loaded with EMP rounds. Specialist Sheldon had briefed her on tactics for combined machine forces—very different from the smaller patrols they'd encountered. The largest combat mechs with aircraft support that Anom saved for full-scale battles. Aircraft strikes were highly effective if the Republic couldn't take them down early with grav-tanks.

Iona felt the hovercraft touch down. The rear hatch opened.

"Plans have changed," Vinden said quietly before they left. "We're launching the attack now—we've been spotted. Further communication will follow on the correct channels."

Iona ran down the ramp, placing a helmet on her head that would let her hear the sergeant's commands during battle. Following the others, she saw a full company of soldiers disembarking from similar hovercraft. Behind them were grav-tanks. She heard jet-copters covering their advance from above. Parts of the forest around their craft had already caught fire from initial grav-tank and aircraft rounds. Iona used her awareness to keep tabs on squad members.

A combat mech rose from the ground in front of her. She stepped back to avoid falling into the sinkhole that formed when it climbed from below. Staring up at the behemoth—this mech was over two stories high instead of the height of two men like the patrol models—Iona reached out with her awareness to locate its processing core. It was in the cockpit-like structure above the main body. The ground shook as the mech advanced, firing on a grav-tank. Rounds hit the tank and Iona moved quickly to dodge flying debris.

Vinden and Pennington turned to cover Laney and Sheldon as they launched grappling hooks onto the mech's main body. Iona followed. Instead of a grappling hook, she threw her grav-disc and broke it into three step-like platforms. She held them at successive elevations with her awareness. As she stepped on one and leapt to the next, the lowest platform pulled through the air to become the next step.

She arrived at the main body simultaneously with the two soldiers and pulled the grav-disc pieces back into her palm. Sheldon moved toward the processing core housing and placed detonation charges from an ammo pouch.

Round panels near it opened. Small metallic beetles swarmed Sheldon. She dropped the detonator and toppled over the mech's edge. Iona heard her yell. She tried reaching out with awareness to slow Sheldon's fall. The swarming beetles broke her concentration. She couldn't assist.

Iona's heart sank as she heard Sheldon's body hit the ground below. With her awareness, she crumpled the metallic beetles trying to cover her own body.

In her helmet's speakers, she heard Vinden command them to jump. The mech was targeting another grav-tank that had moved forward. Vinden had recovered Sheldon's detonator. PFC Laney was beside Iona, scrambling to his feet. Beetles covered him, biting and injecting sleeping agent. Iona grabbed Laney and rolled over the mech's edge. This time she slowed their descent with her awareness. As they hit the ground, she destroyed the remaining beetles that followed.

"Run!" Vinden bellowed.

Pennington helped Iona drag Laney to safety. Side-guns on the mech aimed at their retreat. Before Vinden could press the detonator, rounds ripped open his chest. He staggered and slumped to the ground, pressing the detonator as he fell.

The mech exploded brilliantly, raining debris and scorching flames. The legs fell like felled metallic trees. The sound rang in their ears. Pennington moved to reach Sheldon's position, but flames covered the area, growing by the minute from burning underbrush.

With grim determination, Pennington stood over Vinden. She dropped to her knees to try stopping the bleeding, but it was already too late. He stared up with a blank expression. She pulled off his helmet and closed his eyes.

"We must not let their deaths be in vain." Pennington motioned for Iona and Laney to follow as she moved toward a grav-tank ahead.

Iona surveyed the battlefield. The rest of the platoon had similar success. Drones and mechs fell to combined firepower, but not without other casualties. She smelled burnt flesh. Behind the grav-tank, she heard wounded soldiers crying. Even if they routed the machine forces, this would be a hard-fought victory.

To Iona, it felt like only a couple hours had passed. She'd seen fellow Shapers die over the years on missions, but never been involved in a battle this size. She felt numb standing beside Corporal Pennington.

+ · · · +

Ten hours had gone by. The company had completed their mission. The victory didn't make Iona feel better—she'd witnessed numerous deaths and tried helping as many wounded soldiers recovered from the battlefield as possible. They were back at their starting position now. Pennington had retrieved personal identification chips from both Sheldon and Vinden. She rolled them in her right hand, staring across the landscape.

"They didn't die in vain," Iona said, placing a hand on the corporal's shoulder.

"I know. Doesn't make their loss any easier."

Pennington ordered them to prepare for departure. The soldiers couldn't stay long after destroying the underground factories and guarding forces. Anom would send another force to stop their escape or aircraft for revenge.

The ground around Iona's left foot began shifting. She reached out with her awareness. She had to be cautious about energy usage now—her Chrominthium Core was half full from battle exertion.

Below ground was a tube-shaped machine no bigger than combat drones. Metallic tentacles sprouted, grabbing her leg. When they grabbed—three tentacles about the diameter of paracord—tiny mandibles on their undersides bit into her. The same sleeping agent the beetles had used flowed into her bloodstream. With her awareness, she tried altering its composition. Iona felt groggy, having only altered enough to barely stay awake. Another tentacle covered her head with a pouch.

Almost in unison, Pennington and Laney pulled out combat knives and began hacking at tentacles. The tentacles pulled tighter. All around them as far as they could see, more tentacles erupted, trying to grab as many soldiers as possible. In her helmet comm system, Iona heard the platoon commander order everyone to board nearby personnel carriers. Another wave of aircraft was inbound. Escape and regroup was critical.

As if the tentacles had heard the order, they pulled the soldiers they'd latched onto underground. Iona closed her eyes as she was hauled through layers of earth. She stopped holding her breath when she noticed oxygen being pumped into the pouch covering her head. She could hear muffled cries of other soldiers brought along with her.

Iona pulled back her awareness, not wanting to waste more Chrominthium Core energy, and succumbed to the sleeping agent.

+ · · · +

The tentacle machines pulled their victims to an underground cavern. Worker drones sealed and reinforced the tunnel breaches as the last victims arrived.

A robot designed like a man stood in the cavern's center with a pleased expression.

"More subjects for me to experiment with. My Octupi did well." Indefinite looked at his tentacled machines like a proud father. His metallic body gleamed from the lights on the machines he'd designed. Before launching them when Anom had warned of battle on the network, Indefinite had just finished polishing himself. "Well, I can't waste time admiring myself and my work."

After ordering his machines to continue to the labs he'd constructed to accommodate more human bodies, another human appeared—dressed in the same black suit Exen had worn.

"Oh, how fun this will be."

Grin still on his face, he sat in his hovercar and set the autopilot to drive him back to his labs. He had important work to do and couldn't delay further. Indefinite began humming as his car took off. He leaned back and placed his hands behind his head.

This was his purpose. Rescuing his creators from that damnable Anom.

Chapter 14

After arriving at the Nameless enclave, Exen was made to wait in a tent. Perpetual mist covered the valley and a mountain stream ran through its center. Under different circumstances, Exen would have had no problem falling asleep to the sound of flowing water. The tent was large enough for four people to sleep comfortably. Simple construction, practical layout.

Exen began nodding off and fought to stay awake. It had been too long since he'd had a full night's rest. After the surgery, he hadn't felt the same—like his mind had been dragged across sandpaper, light enough to avoid damage but enough to cause constant irritation.

As if sensing his condition, three of the Nameless entered his tent bringing food and water. They bowed and left the provisions on a small wooden table, then departed without speaking.

A different figure entered alone. This was odd—Exen hadn't seen any of them travel alone before. They always moved in groups of three. Instead of a brown robe, this one wore gray.

Exen stood, but the figure raised a hand suggesting he remain comfortable.

"Do not trouble yourself, Exen." A deep masculine voice, clear and unimpeded by telepathy. "You must rest and regain your strength. Much will be required of you. This much we have seen." The figure reached within his robes and pulled out a square black device that fit in his palm. "The others in this village call me an oracle, one of the voices for the Nameless. You may call me Dmitri."

Dmitri closed his eyes. A light on the device's side activated. He placed it against Exen's temple. "Do not be alarmed. You will feel pain similar to when the others freed you from Anom's control, but afterward you will feel great relief."

Exen sat and placed his hands on his knees, preparing himself. The light on the device began pulsing. Pain hit him like a hot needle puncturing through one side of his head straight through to the other. He fought the urge to claw at his temples.

Dmitri powered down the device. Blood trickled from Exen's nose, followed by two pebble-sized nodes. They hit the tent floor and Dmitri crushed them with a bare foot. His foot wasn't scrawny like the other Nameless—the skin on his hands and feet was tan and healthy.

"Do you feel better?" Dmitri asked. He lowered his hood.

Exen stared. Dmitri looked like a normal human. Long brown hair, a goatee with occasional gray strands, and brilliant green eyes. No distorted features, no fused mouth, no sunken eye sockets.

"Ah yes, I am an oracle, Exen, not one of the Nameless. We are a rare occurrence among them. Only a handful are born each generation."

Questions flooded Exen's mind. These people seemed so simple—like nomads traveling across Earth's uninhabited regions—but the technology he'd witnessed and the advanced telepathic capabilities of the Nameless were astounding.

"I will tell you of our people," Dmitri said, as if reading Exen's thoughts. "But first, let us eat. You need sustenance after what you've endured."

Dmitri gestured to the food the Nameless had brought. Exen realized he was starving. They ate in silence for several minutes before Dmitri began explaining.

Over the next hour, Dmitri told Exen about the Nameless. When he finished, he excused himself to attend to important matters, promising to return soon.

Exen sat cross-legged on a blanket he'd unrolled and processed what he'd learned.

The Nameless were a failed experiment conducted by the original Haeolt Collective. The Collective had even tried purging them when results didn't match expectations. But the people used for experimentation were indigenous to a region on the South American continent. When some escaped the research facility after learning genocide orders had been issued, they had no trouble hiding in mountain caverns.

A decade or two passed. It seemed the Collective no longer hunted them. They waited additional years to ensure it wasn't a ploy, then finally sent scouts. The scouts found a devastated world.

When the Final Wars were fought, the Nameless had only been slightly modified by Collective experiments—telepathic abilities and a type of sixth sense they couldn't label. But after generations of isolation in caverns and changes in diet, they gradually became what they were today. The oracles theorized that residual contamination from weapons of mass destruction might have contributed to their current physiology.

Only in the last century had the Nameless ventured from the caverns and started establishing enclaves to prepare for what they called "the day of Reckoning." Dmitri had been careful to explain that most oracles didn't share the Nameless belief in this prophecy. The Nameless had a collective ideology the oracles couldn't fully understand—spiritual or religious in nature. As oracles, they guided the Nameless when allowed, but they were more scientists than prophets.

Exen found all this intriguing. He was pleased to have encountered the Nameless. He'd do his best to enlist their aid. They had no love for the Haeolt Collective. If he formed a stronger bond with Dmitri, he might convince them to ally with the Order of Infinity.

Exen lay down on the blanket, thinking about his conversation with Dmitri, and fell asleep.

+ · · · +

"Wake up, Exen."

Exen sat upright, embarrassed he'd drifted off so easily.

"I hate to wake you when you finally achieved rest," Dmitri said, "but we've found your friend's location." The relaxed expression Dmitri usually wore had vanished. A scowl darkened his face. "If we move quickly, I can help you rescue her before she's deep within one of Anom's monoliths."

During their earlier conversation, Dmitri had explained how the Nameless discovered the terraforming AI after Anom captured several of them and dragged them into monoliths. Since that day, they'd carefully monitored machine movements and surviving human factions. The oracles had wanted to reach out to other humans, but the Nameless collectively forbid this action. They no longer pressed the idea.

The Nameless despised the monoliths. They'd even knocked one down when it was constructed too close to one of their hidden enclaves.

Exen was beginning to understand the oracles' position better—more diplomats than rulers, more advisors than leaders. The Nameless made decisions collectively through their telepathic connection. The oracles guided them when they listened.

On the way to rescue Iona, Exen would need to reconsider his approach to forming an alliance. The Nameless seemed deeply spiritual, possibly superstitious. If he wasn't careful, they might reject the Order of Infinity as well. He definitely didn't want them as enemies if the Order was to continue operating on Earth.

Exen followed Dmitri from the tent. They boarded a skiff parked outside—smaller than the one Exen had ridden before, with no visible weapons.

"Hold on, Exen. It won't be long before we reach our destination."

Exen crouched and gripped the skiff's side, peering over its edge. The vessel lifted from the ground. The peaceful feeling from earlier left him. Now he felt only determination.

With Dmitri's help and the Nameless's intervention, he'd freed himself from Indefinite's oppression. He was still an altered version of his previous self—half human, half machine—but now he had complete control of his mind and body.

Time to rejoin forces with Iona. They'd continue their original mission of investigating humanity's birth world. So much to tell their brothers and sisters of the Order.

Exen smiled at Dmitri. Dmitri nodded in return. The skiff accelerated, moving much faster than his previous journey. Exen calmed his mind as they flew through the mist-covered valley toward Iona's location.

Chapter 15

After a day of replicating his partitions as fast as possible throughout the network, Cytar found his mind expanding. He could process data faster than before—even though his computation nodes as a Haeolt Collective member had given him an edge over most humans, this was different. The network integration allowed him to infiltrate Anom's systems on a far grander scale. He processed video feeds from multiple machine patrols simultaneously and mapped exact dimensions of Anom's facilities in real time.

Thousands of Anom's monoliths covered Earth's surface, each with corresponding underground complexes. The network was streamed from satellites in orbit. Anom also had a presence on the moon—hundreds of factories and a spaceport ready to launch capital ships powered by hyperspace capable jump drives. Each capital ship could carry squadrons of frigates, five cruisers, two battlecruisers, and one battleship. When Cytar discovered the lunar facilities, he accessed a databank showing exactly how many ships Anom needed to complete before attacking Leondricidus without considerable loss.

Cytar knew he had to make his move soon. First, he needed to find a way to contact the Delegation of Six. He continued working on his virus and reached out to a combat drone squad closest to his scout ship. The ship hadn't been discovered by Anom yet. Cytar no longer needed to transfer into machines to control them—his expanded consciousness could command them directly through the network. He sent a masked command and watched through one of the squad's drones. They'd reach his ship in approximately thirty minutes.

When the squad reached his scout ship, Cytar looped patrol footage to avoid drawing Anom's attention. The spacecraft remained under stealth, but the field would collapse when he accessed it. Through the drone he'd been using for observation, he took direct control. Instead of the laborious process from before, controlling it now felt like lifting a finger to push a button. He moved the drone to hover beside the control pad. A panel opened on the drone and a tether module extended, pressing the control panel and opening the hatch.

Cytar was pleased to find his ship intact. He used the drone's data link to access it and upload a message. After successfully transmitting it through hyperspace to Leondricidus, he attached the drone to the pilot's chair and sent a message back through the network reporting the drone as faulty and requiring repairs. He commanded the rest of the squad to return to their assigned patrol route.

Cytar powered up his scout ship and lifted it from the ground through his network connection. He needed to hide it away from possible conflict. Reports on the network indicated humans—survivors from the Final Wars—had attacked hundreds of monoliths hiding factory facilities. Cytar accessed database maps and found a ravine about five hundred miles from the ships current location. Far enough from any of Anom's facilities, with no patrol routes through it. He programmed the coordinates into the navigator controls and it took off. By the time it reached the ravine, his virus would be ready to launch.

This would be the perfect moment for the virus to achieve full effect. The chaos the surviving humans had created by assaulting the factories was favorable indeed. With the scout ship safely hidden in the ravine and placed in power-saving mode, Cytar released his virus into the network.

The virus was designed to resemble other programs Anom routinely used. After other memory cores and processing centers copied the program—if it wasn't discovered soon enough—Cytar would seize the opportunity to infiltrate Anom's main processing core. He'd located its position: where the Haeolt Collective's terraforming pod had initially landed. Once inside the main core, he'd rewrite the AI to give himself complete control of everything Anom had created.

He just needed to wait patiently for a day or two. The virus should work. Anom was overconfident and thought little of human capabilities—even augmented ones like Cytar's. He was proud of the virus he'd created. While waiting to see if it would accomplish his goal, Cytar continued expanding his consciousness throughout Anom's networks, preparing for the moment when he'd seize control.

Chapter 16

Parking his hovercar in a designated spot he'd created, Indefinite opened the door and leaped out. He couldn't keep the excitement from showing on his face as he hurried down a side corridor leading to his labs. His new subjects would already be placed on operating tables under substantial doses of anesthetics. He'd thought of many improvements from his first experiment on the human named Exen and looked forward to implementing most of them.

The corridor itself had been decorated with symbols and deities from Greek mythology. Whereas Anom had no interest in humanity's history, Indefinite found everything about them fascinating. The Great Empires from antiquity intrigued him most, especially those that worshipped many gods. They seemed the most eccentric and produced the best historical stories. He particularly liked the Iliad and the Odyssey. He looked forward to writing his own stories from this period—becoming a type of Homer, putting his own flair on tales after achieving his purpose.

When he left the corridor and arrived at his labs, Indefinite admired his new laboratory. Decent size, with four separate chambers. One chamber was reserved for his experiments on humanity. The others were for future experiments he was planning. He'd also kept his labs secret from Anom by reprogramming robots he'd retrieved from the Fueridi Research Installation. With their help, he'd built a new network to relay commands to his workers—one he'd eventually replace Anom's network with.

It was only a matter of time before he planted the bomb he was secretly making into Anom's central processing center. He'd found the locations where Anom had secured backup copies of his consciousness, and other explosives were being prepared as well.

Fortunately, the AI hadn't placed backups on the moon or other planets in the nearby solar system.

Indefinite stood beside one of his operating tables and looked down at the subject—a male soldier from the Orsen Republic. His uniform had been shredded while traveling from surface to tunnels below. Several abrasions and cuts marked his face and hands. His wrists and ankles were bound. Indefinite checked to ensure the robots had properly connected the medical equipment. Everything was set up correctly. He smiled and moved down the row of tables.

There were one hundred tables total in this chamber. He paused to check his own databank to locate where they'd placed the human not dressed like the other Republic members. The female Shaper was three rows ahead of his current position. He whistled as he walked to her table and stood beside her, placing a hand on her shoulder.

"Do not worry," Indefinite said as if the woman could hear him. "I've improved my technique. I won't have to alter your face like I did to your friend. I've also figured out how to ensure you won't betray me like he did."

The constant grin he wore was gone. Instead, disgust crossed his features as he thought of losing control of Exen. Anom hadn't mentioned it yet. Indefinite hoped he was too busy dealing with the attacks the Republic and its allies had orchestrated. It would give Indefinite enough time to operate on this human and the others—prove they were still a valuable resource.

"Where are you, Indefinite?" Anom's voice came from a speaker drone back in his personal chambers. Indefinite had set up a direct link from his chamber to his network. He still answered to Anom and had to be careful how he proceeded.

"I'm currently examining the damage the feral apes have caused," Indefinite lied. "Do you need my assistance?"

"Yes. Something is wrong. Report to my battle headquarters at once."

"I'll be there as soon as possible, Anom."

Indefinite heard the change in tone in Anom's last sentence. It wavered, as if something was interfering with his ability to speak. Maybe this would be his chance to rid this planet of Anom. He moved his hand from the Shaper's shoulder and brushed his hand through her hair. As he walked back toward the corridor leading to his hover car, Indefinite issued commands for his work to begin with some procedures he'd planned to do himself. He didn't have time to begin them with Anom's request. Even though he wanted to perform them personally, time was critical. He had to prove to Anom these creatures were worth the trouble. He wanted to ensure his final alterations were perfect before operating on the Shaper. He couldn't afford to lose her like he'd lost Exen.

As Indefinite sat in his hover car and set coordinates for Anom's battle headquarters, he began whistling. Everything was falling into place. He felt he was achieving his purpose—rescuing humanity from itself. All he had to do now was replace Anom and take over the grand empire he'd built. The infrastructure would give him the ability to launch fleets into space and find the rest of intergalactic humanity so he could improve them. They'd done a fine job creating him. He only wanted to return the favor.

+ · · · +

During the drive, Indefinite surveyed the damage from the last assault the Orsen Republic launched. Rubble at many sites that had hidden underground factories Anom used to build his machine armies. Parts of forests burned to the ground. Destroyed drones and mechs lay interspersed with human corpses.

As fast as they'd attacked and destroyed their intended targets, the Republic had disappeared. Indefinite admired their ingenuity. For the last two centuries, many human factions left on Earth had tried waging war against Anom. They'd all met bitter defeat and hadn't achieved the level of success the Orsen Republic and its allies had. He wondered if this was why Anom was shaken and complaining something was wrong. Maybe the AI was having second thoughts about his supposed self-importance. Indefinite was sure he'd find a way to take advantage of the situation.

While lowering his hover car, Indefinite pressed a button on the dash that opened a communication line with Anom. "I'm here as you requested, Anom."

When the hover car rested on the ground near a monolith, a door opened in the structure.

"You...must...hurry..." Anom said over the comm line.

Indefinite noticed the tone again. He put on a worried expression—one he'd practiced countless times to appear believable when being dishonest—and walked to the monolith's entrance.

A grav-lift awaited—just large enough for one person. The lift took off as soon as he stepped on. The hallway was similar to all other monoliths he'd visited. When he took over, he'd liven things up and try different architectural designs from humanity's history.

The first thing that would have to go would be these damned monoliths. He was beginning to despise them as much as he despised Anom. Earth was beckoning for human cities to dot its landscape once again. This was their birth homeworld, not the property of some crazed AI that had found fault with those who created him. Indefinite guessed Anom was a product from humanity. It was possible an alien faction had sent him to seek revenge on the intergalactic human community. But it was more likely some human faction wanted to regain control of a reborn Earth for their own purposes.

The grav-lift took off, then skidded to a sudden stop. Indefinite steadied himself to avoid falling. The lift took off again. This wasn't usual. Something wasn't right. Indefinite was unsure what he'd face when brought to whatever room Anom was summoning him to. The grav-lift traveled down three hallways, then up a lift tube.

Whereas humans would have lit their buildings—especially when calling guests—Anom's facilities were pitch black. Indefinite didn't like the atmosphere at all. He disliked using the infrared spectrum of his optics. It reminded him he was just a robot and not like his creators. He liked thinking of himself as human whenever possible, even though he knew he couldn't delude himself into believing it was true. A human could have done the same thing he was attempting—another aspect he found fascinating. With the right suggestive psychotherapy, a human could believe it was a machine or some other creature. Maybe one day he'd have one of them create an organic body he could place his processing core into.

The grav-lift traveled twelve stories up the tube, then stopped at the top floor. Indefinite had already uploaded schematics from Anom's databanks, wanting to know the layout of the room he'd be walking into. He wasn't sure if Anom was truly in distress or about to test his loyalty. He'd have to be ready to escape if the AI had figured out his purpose.

The grav-lift left the tube. Indefinite stepped into the security room. He heard several scanners activate, then the pressure release of the door seal on the opposite side.

He entered the room Anom had designated as his strategic battle headquarters. He found it ironic that Anom had an actual room for issuing commands during wartime. Rather human of him. The room was large enough to fit hundreds of monitors hovering in the air. On the monitors in front of the entrance, he noticed symbols and a language he didn't understand.

As Indefinite stepped closer, he realized they weren't unrecognized symbols or an unknown language. It was gibberish. The letters were repeating consonants of computer language. The symbols were distorted computations. Something had infiltrated Anom's system and infected it.

This was fortunate timing. Indefinite approached the monitors, analyzing the corruption patterns. Whatever had done this was sophisticated—far more sophisticated than anything the surviving human factions could create. Someone else was making a move against Anom. The question was whether Indefinite could use this to his advantage before whoever launched this attack completed their objective.

Chapter 17

On the way to rescue Iona, Dmitri told Exen how another group of Nameless had placed a tracker on the hover car and followed when Indefinite took off. As soon as the vehicle stopped, the Nameless followed the robot to a hidden laboratory. They didn't have to infiltrate the lab to know Iona was there—they could sense her psyche in their proximity.

"They told me it was the same sensation when they found you, only fainter." Dmitri had slowed the skiff and looped around a grove of beech trees. The trees were at the top of a hill. On the back side was a slope that looked recently made. Grass was present but much shorter than the grass surrounding the hilltop.

When the skiff stopped behind the grove, it changed color to match nearby foliage. Dmitri stepped off and walked halfway down the slope. He motioned for Exen to stand next to him. When Exen arrived, Dmitri pulled out a small cylindrical device. He knelt and hummed softly. The device lit up and illuminated writing on its side. Exen couldn't make out the writing. After Dmitri finished humming, the cylinder spun in his hands. A faint square outline formed around where they stood, then the ground shifted. It lowered. After they descended about ten meters, another metal square slid into place at the surface.

Every three meters on either side of the corridor they were descending through were round green lights. Exen found the lighting odd. What kind of AI would go to the trouble of colored lights to illuminate an elevator shaft? It didn't seem like Anom's work. He hoped it was the work of that damned robot with the peculiar grin. Exen's primary goal was helping Iona, but if Indefinite was down here, he'd be happy to put him out of service.

"We're getting closer," Dmitri whispered. "Iona's psyche is pulsing. She must be un-conscious."

"We must hurry then." Exen's jaw tightened. "I'm afraid that same machine has plans to operate on her as well."

The lift stopped at the bottom of the passageway. They were in a room that opened into three other corridors. The room itself was empty. Dmitri moved toward the corridor on the west side. He lowered his hood and closed his eyes while moving his hands in a similar pattern Exen had seen the other Nameless use. Dmitri stopped and opened his eyes.

"Iona is somewhere beyond this corridor." Dmitri turned from Exen and walked at a brisk pace into the corridor. Exen followed close behind and readied his awareness. He was sure Indefinite wouldn't be pleased to see him after the oracle had freed him from the neural inhibitor. Both he and Dmitri would have to be quick if Indefinite had a sizable security force protecting his "patients."

+ · · · +

Not the outcome Indefinite had wanted. He walked as fast as he could from the lift to his hover car. The sun was behind the monolith, casting a shadow on his vehicle. He should have taken the chance at controlling Anom. It was sure to end with him also being infected, but if he'd succeeded...

The door opened when he approached. Indefinite sat in his vehicle. Without delay, he took off at high speed heading back toward his laboratory.

"Indefinite," a metallic, nasally voice said over the hovercar's speaker system. "There are intruders in your laboratory. I tried contacting you earlier with no success and have proceeded to have them followed."

"Chumley, why haven't you apprehended them?" Indefinite wondered if he should have programmed Chumley with more intelligence. He'd programmed him at a basic AI level, wanting a being that could oversee things when he wasn't there. Indefinite was afraid if he programmed Chumley more like himself, he'd also be scheming to get rid of Indefinite—just like he was trying to overthrow Anom.

"The only reason I haven't sent the others to stop them is because it's only two and they haven't reached your main chambers yet. Also, one of them is a strange-looking human and the other is Exen."

"Good work, Chumley. I'll be there as soon as possible. If they get too close to the main chambers, stall them as long as you can. I want them unharmed."

"Will do, Indefinite."

Indefinite heard the line close and turned the autopilot on. It wouldn't take long to reach his laboratory. He was looking forward to assimilating Exen again. This time, though, he'd place an improved neural inhibitor system—one that didn't need the first node he'd used, only an adjustment to the psychic accelerator he'd found inside Exen's head.

+ · · · +

Exen followed Dmitri down the long corridor. After half a mile of straight passage, it began curving slightley.

"We're close," Dmitri said. "Her presence grows stronger."

The corridor emptied into a long hallway. He saw a door ahead. Decorations covered the door. As they approached, Exen realized they were pictographs. He wasn't sure what they represented, but they weren't the interweaving animal sequences Anom used.

"Not behind this one," Dmitri said while quietly removing his hand from the door. He turned and continued down the hallway, passing two more doors before stopping at the last one.

Exen scanned with his awareness at the hallway's end. He grabbed Dmitri and pulled him backward as a sequence of darts fired from wall panels. Exen scanned the darts that hit the floor behind them. The chemical compound wasn't lethal—it was designed to dull their senses.

All four doors in the hallway opened. Out stepped what appeared to be soldiers from the Orsen Republic. Exen knew better. Three soldiers from the closest door all had glazed-over eyes. One of the three had an arm enhanced with metal components.

"You do not have to resist," a voice said over the intercom system. "Indefinite only wants to assist humans like you and help improve on your initial design."

"Who is he to say we aren't capable of this on our own?" Exen said. Both he and Dmitri stood back to back, ready to fight. "If he desires to help us, why is he friends with Anom? We will see to Indefinite and Anom's demise."

"I was afraid of this," the voice said.

As if the voice going silent was a signal to attack, the enhanced soldiers advanced on Exen and Dmitri. Exen dodged the first one's grasp and moved to the side of the second. He used his awareness to locate the neural inhibitors and cognition imprinters on the soldiers. Finding them, he carefully collapsed the devices' sides on themselves, trying not to harm surrounding brain tissue. All three soldiers fell to the ground. Other soldiers from the doors moved to replace them.

"Go assist Iona." Dmitri had already lowered his hood and raised his hands. He began moving them in a different repeating pattern than Exen had seen before. "I will stall them as long as necessary."

Exen turned from Dmitri and entered the door. In front of him were rows of operating tables with men and women soldiers in different states of operation. Some seemed finished—already sewn up with their augmentations. Others, to Exen's astonishment, were being cut open by robots similar to Indefinite's appearance. Blood and organs littered the floor. Toward the back were soldiers that hadn't been touched. He saw Iona laying on one of the tables. She was bound and still unconscious.

He projected his awareness farther and scanned Iona. He let out a sigh of relief—she hadn't been touched.

Time to accomplish what they came here for. He crossed the rows and stood beside Iona, pushing a button on a nearby panel that released her wrists and ankles. Iona opened her eyes and sat upright.

"I was waiting for the right moment to act," Iona said while sliding off the table to stand next to Exen. "Did my best to make my vital signs appear like I was under."

"Now is the time." Exen reached out and touched her arm. She returned the touch and placed her hand where the metal plate was. The two of them were close. On previous occasions, they'd almost crossed the relationship boundaries they'd put in place to stay professional. But now it was as if Iona and Exen had gone further than that. Through their connection, he felt her awareness of his pain—the deep ache of being part machine and human.

A door that had previously been hidden irised outward. The sound of it hissing caused Exen and Iona to face its direction. A robot stepped through. Although he was similar to the ones in the laboratory, there was something deeper about the expression on his face.

"Indefinite," Exen said. He stepped forward and rendered one of the empty operating tables into pieces with his awareness. He shaped the pieces into miniature spears and thrust the bulk of them in Indefinite's direction. The remaining pieces he sent into a nearby robot fast approaching their location. They connected with the robot's torso and it toppled backward with a shower of sparks.

"Is this how you welcome me?" Indefinite waited until the spears were close, then faster than Exen anticipated, rolled to the left. One piece caught Indefinite's right arm and pinned him against the wall. "And you show up uninvited only to offer violence as I enter my home. How rude. I thought you had better manners than that, Exen, especially for one who carries the title of Shaper."

Indefinite pulled the spear from his arm and retrieved a pistol from a side compartment on one of his legs. The pistol gleamed brilliantly like the rest of his body. He moved toward Exen. As Indefinite closed in on Exen and Iona's position, eight other robots joined from different directions. Behind those came augmented soldiers.

Exen pulled the spears back to orbit him and Iona and changed them into razor-sharp pieces no bigger than grains of sand. Indefinite raised his hand. The robots nearby stopped advancing.

"Let's see how ethical you are," Indefinite said. He was grinning and placed the pistol back in its compartment. He crossed both arms, one hand stroking his chin. "You might be rude, but I'm sure your heart is at least in the right place."

The robots separated farther apart. The soldiers began advancing. Exen didn't want to harm them. If they tried to apprehend him and Iona, the shards would rip them apart. There were more than ten, and Exen didn't know if he could deactivate all of them in time.

"Work on the robots," Exen said. "I'll do what I can to override the soldiers."

Iona nodded. When Exen dropped the pieces that were orbiting them and acting as a shield, she projected onto the two robots that were closest. She stirred the air molecules around one and pushed it into the other. When they collided, Iona collapsed the servo housings in their joints. They both tumbled to the ground, limbs intertwined like discarded rag dolls. She moved closer and pulled back with the air molecules she'd projected earlier, beheading both robots. Redirecting the inertia from that movement, she tore their torsos in half.

Exen dropped to his knees to avoid a swing from another robot and reached out with his awareness, trying to target the advancing soldiers. He was only able to destroy the neural inhibitors and cognition imprinters on six of them. The other four reached him and had a firm grasp on his arms and legs. Exen tried again to use his awareness to alter the soldiers holding him, but something was blocking it.

Off to his right side, he heard a chuckle. Indefinite was holding a round device in his hands, similar to a Chrominthium Core but larger.

"After experimenting on you the first time," Indefinite said as he stepped closer to Exen, "I figured there was a way to block the signals your psychic accelerator projected. Glad to find out I was right."

Exen tried again to push with his awareness, desperate to wipe that stupid grin from Indefinite's face. This time, sharp pain erupted inside his head.

"Don't try too hard," Indefinite said. "I wouldn't want you to hurt yourself."

He laughed. Iona rushed forward, charging into Indefinite. The device flew from his hand. Both Indefinite and Iona tumbled to the ground. She rolled away before he could latch onto her, knowing his strength was probably far greater than hers. She crushed the device under the heel of her boot.

Indefinite stood. His grin vanished, replaced by something darker. His metallic features contorted with what looked like rage.

"No longer am I here to play games. Destroy them."

Indefinite raised his arm. Other soldiers rose from the tables. Some weren't even close to being finished with their augmentations, but with her awareness, Iona noticed they'd been pumped full of adrenaline and painkillers. Too many approached. She tried doing what Exen had done, but she didn't know the layout of the nodes within the soldiers' heads. Before she could map out their heads with her awareness and know what to alter without causing damage, a group dogpiled onto her.

Seeing Iona's situation, Exen fought the pain in his head and now in his arms and legs—the soldiers were trying to rip his limbs from their sockets after Indefinite's commands. He found he was unable to use his awareness to stop them. The last exertion had been too much. His Chrominthium Core was now in shutdown mode due to dangerous psychic strain. He could override the safety procedures, but the result would likely cause permanent damage to his psyche, potentially fragmenting his consciousness beyond repair.

The soldiers beside Exen released their hold. They clutched the sides of their heads. Puzzled, Exen looked at Iona, but he couldn't sense her using her awareness. Then he saw that the other soldiers near her fell backward.

"Thankfully, some of my kin showed up to assist us," Dmitri said as he, along with a small group of Nameless, entered the room. "I did tell them where we were going before I left, but I thought they might have other plans."

They must survive to face the Reckoning, the Nameless said telepathically in unison so that both Exen and Iona could hear them. *Without them we have no chance of surviving what is fated to come from the void.*

"I don't know about this Reckoning of theirs," Iona said as she brushed dirt from her Shaper suit, "but I'm glad it involves us not falling to these machines."

The Nameless reached within their robes and pulled out laser pistols. Dmitri had a resonance blade in his right hand. Working in conjunction with the Nameless, they made quick work of the remaining robots.

Indefinite stood cowering in one of the room's corners. He acted like someone about to be unjustly accused of high treason. Exen and Iona crossed the room, trying not to step on fallen soldiers. Dmitri and the Nameless followed closely behind. One of the Nameless was tending to soldiers bleeding from wounds not properly sewn before being put into commission by Indefinite.

"Whatever your plans were," Exen said as he reached to take the resonance blade from Dmitri, "they end today."

Indefinite was now groveling on the ground.

"Please, I beg of you. I only meant to help."

Two of the Nameless moved to Indefinite's sides and picked him up to a kneeling position. Exen brought the resonance blade above his head. The blade hummed, its edge shimmering with harmonic distortion. With unbridled fury, he lowered it. The blade passed through Indefinite's neck without resistance, dissolving molecular bonds in its path. The head separated cleanly and rolled across the floor. Despite his turn of fortune, the stupid grin he almost always wore appeared back on Indefinite's face.

"No worries. You will see in the end, my purpose shall be accomplished."

The lights that powered his eyes went out. The Nameless fired their pistols at the robot's head, ensuring it was destroyed.

"We don't think Anom has knowledge of this place," Dmitri said as Exen gave him back his resonance blade. "But if he does, we should move quickly to assist what soldiers have survived and get them out of here."

"Agreed." Exen moved to help the Nameless. Iona followed after gathering her thoughts for a brief moment.

Destroying Indefinite had been a challenge, but as the two of them tended to one of the soldiers, they exchanged glances. They could see in each other's eyes that they acknowledged this was only one small battle in a war they'd have to engage in to rid Earth of the rest of the machine menace.

Chapter 18

One of the last original members who had formed the Haeolt Collective, Thomas Haeolt, sat in his hover chair looking at displays containing news of recent events. His chair was silver-plated with other precious metals woven in, and many jewels outlined the armrests. The chair wasn't just ornate and worthy of display—it was practical. Within were all the systems necessary to keep Thomas Haeolt alive. He was on his forty-eighth clone. Each successive clone over the years based on his DNA had been less capable, even to the point of being nearly immobile after creation. At least their minds didn't follow the same pattern of degradation.

The only clones that had achieved near perfection were those of the Wraith program. Thomas had the only scientist who developed the technology put to death. The scientist had been his brother, Orthello Haeolt, who'd tricked Thomas into believing he'd given him all the results from his research.

Knowing how his brother disliked him and only kept him around for furthering the profits of Haeolt Interstellar Flight Co., Orthello had given him false records that seemed like suitable plans for replicating the Wraith program's clone technology. It wasn't until several generations after Thomas and those loyal to him had started uploading their consciousness into a flawed cloning procedure that they discovered Orthello had deceived them.

The process wasn't in the cloning procedure itself but in how the original specimens' DNA were augmented. That was why the Haeolt Collective could keep producing top-tier clones for those who'd been part of that program, and why they were selective with how lesser members of the Collective were allowed to breed.

Moving his hover chair from the displays, Thomas steered toward the back wall of his strategic planning room. At the back was a lift tube. He crossed the room and hovered over the platform that would lead him to where the Delegation of Six waited.

For countless millennia, the Haeolt Collective thought they were ruled by a benevolent council full of wise beings who only thought of the group as a whole. Little did they know it was a carefully fashioned ruse—that Thomas Haeolt was the supreme dictator over the Collective and their homeworld of Leondricidus.

More than twenty-five hundred years ago, Thomas had gotten rid of all who opposed him and made it mandatory that all who stayed on Leondricidus join the Haeolt Collective. All others were told they were allowed to leave. Videos had even been made showing them depart. The videos were real enough, but Thomas made sure no one saw evidence of them being blown into pieces by a mercenary fleet he'd stationed at their first jump point. He couldn't be too careful with outsiders learning specifics of the Collective's procedures.

If the intergalactic community knew how he operated, he'd be put on trial. But they were too weak to understand true power, even when it operated behind the veil of his supposed Collective. He was pleased with what he'd learned over the last week. His agent on Endrunel had been successful at sabotaging the Order of Infinity.

There wasn't anyone Thomas hated more than Culminas. Culminas's Order had placed him on a pedestal, almost deifying the man. Worse, he'd figured out a cloning procedure superior even to the Wraith program. Of course, the idiot didn't bother capitalizing on the procedure. Thomas only saw this as weakness. Something about it "falling into the wrong hands."

As the platform lowered down the lift tube, Thomas had already decided how he'd handle the next steps of his plans to recover Earth from the terraforming AI that had gone awry. A distant descendant of his, Cytar, had done good work on Earth. Thomas had ordered Armond Telre to eliminate evidence of his sabotage on Endrunel and report back. Other Wraiths were waiting to join Armond as he headed to Earth next to support Cytar.

A clone was being prepared for the disembodied Cytar, and Thomas was leaving it up to Armond to decide if he was worthy of it.

If Cytar failed to gain control of Anom, it might be worth destroying him so no evidence of the Haeolt Collective's involvement in creating Anom was discovered. But it probably wasn't necessary because of the way Thomas had engineered loyalty into

Collective members. Separation sickness was quite ingenious, as was giving them the natural euphoria of improved data requisition.

Of course, all of his plans were going to receive actual input from other members of the Delegation of Six. He'd already programmed what they were going to say during the meeting. Thomas despised robots that looked like humans, but to maintain complete control without fear of rebellion that existed when government was too overbearing, he was happy to play his part as a delegation member. He'd executed enough of humanity at the beginning of his reign. At least this way, he hardly ever had to impose his form of justice on the populace. They loved the Delegation of Six, just as the council itself loved the members of the Collective.

Thomas parked his hover chair in the spot designated for him. In a room as ornate as his chair, the meeting began.

✦ · · ✦

Watching the explosions take place at his observatory and orbital telescope, Armond Telre was overjoyed to find he'd probably survive this mission. Now Thomas Haeolt of the Delegation of Six had ordered him to report back to Leondricidus. He'd travel there as soon as possible, but first he'd have to make it look like his travel logs said he was going to other locations first. Armond knew the Order of Infinity would investigate every possibility to find who had sabotaged them on Endrunel. He couldn't be too careful.

Satisfied he'd done everything correctly, Armond boarded his shuttle that would take him to a travel barge supposed to fly directly to the planet of Shivaln. He was sure the pilot wouldn't mind if the ship took a slight detour and dropped him off at Leondricidus, especially if there was a case of chrominthium involved in the transaction. The Order of Infinity wasn't the only faction that needed the interdimensional alloy. On the black market, it would fetch a pretty sum.

After the shuttle docked in the correct bay, Armond stepped into the passenger facility's main concourse. The space stretched three stories high with translucent panels in the ceiling that let in natural light from Endrunel's sun. Walkways crisscrossed at different levels, and the air hummed with the sound of hundreds of travelers moving between gates. Vendors had set up stalls along the outer walls—colorful awnings and holographic signs advertising everything from Novrin textiles to off-world cuisine.

Armond strolled past a group of businesspeople arguing in Omatrin dialects and tried to find a food vendor. Most long-distance travel barges were full of vendors offering exotic foods, materials, and services. It had been a long time since a Vethalian had given him a back rub or he'd found a vendor with speedle sushi. There was nothing like relaxing while eating a raw delicacy. If he could find both, he'd be in heaven—and that was saying much for a member of a faction that believed the afterlife was only available via clone.

He had five hours before the ship departed. Enough time to find food and relaxation before he needed to bribe the captain. He'd already changed his outfit and hair to make him look like a tourist instead of a serious professor from an observatory. The Order of Infinity would have a hard time figuring out their current conundrum thanks to Armond's handiwork.

Chapter 19

"We need to find Indefinite," Anom said while observing his new avatar form. "He isn't responding when I try to contact him."

The form was that of a man's—still chrome in color with no hair follicles. He found no need to create an exact replica of a human. Five days had passed since Indefinite had eliminated the virus that nearly unraveled Anom. Now Indefinite was nowhere to be found, and Anom wanted him here so he could tell him that he'd been wrong about the feral apes.

Inside his strategic planning room, four other robots—like the one Anom was now "wearing"—sat in chairs around a meeting table. The table was made from ancient oak he had salvaged from a ruined city shortly after beginning Earth's terraforming. Even though he was using the form of those he loathed, Anom reminded himself it served a purpose and wasn't the same kind of odd curiosity Indefinite had about humans. Each of the other robots was identical and contained an innate copy of his vast mind. If Anom perished and couldn't send the correct signal to the robots, one would activate and his AI consciousness would go online.

He paced along the opposite side of the table from where the robots sat and paused to place his hands on the oak surface. He'd waited long enough. Time to accelerate the extinction of those feral apes.

"I was going to wait patiently for the deathblow I wanted to deal humanity—even those far away—but now I can no longer delay."

"You are right, sir," one of the robots in the middle said. "They grow bold in their attacks. If left alone, their resistance will grow stronger."

"Agreed." Anom continued to pace. He didn't know why he liked to pace while in this form, but something about it calmed him.

"They think they've secured a sound victory by destroying some of my factories. They also think they've kept their submersible crafts hidden from me, but I have seen them."

Five displays on suspensor chassis floated over to the table. Satellite images of energy patterns along with underwater footage of the submarines played on a continuous loop. With a thought, Anom changed one display to a live feed from his own submarines. They weren't far from the Orsen Republic fleet. Anom sent a command for them to fire. Within minutes, several of the Republic's submarines were drifting downward. Only a few escape pods were seen leaving within range of Anom's fleet.

"As you can see, whatever plans they had should now be falling apart."

Anom changed the displays to another set of live feeds. Each display now showed footage from tunnelers using infrared spectrum. All had maneuvered close and sent tiny insect drones into the underground military complexes to scout them out. Anom had mapped out each complex and knew where the officers and other important officials resided. Soon he'd have the tunnelers breach the complexes and inject drones and mechs within to exterminate as many humans as possible. After his forces retreated, Anom would collapse the complexes, rendering them useless.

"When they retreat from this attack and gather their forces, I will have a nasty surprise for them. I thought I would never contemplate the use of any weapon that would harm Earth again, but I see I have no other choice."

On the displays, images now showed aircraft taking off. Bomber jets armed with missiles containing nuclear warheads.

"The only way we can be rid of them is to make sure they cannot survive even if a small percentage are left. Time is on the machines' side."

The other robots nodded in unison and sat on the edge of their seats as if in awe of Anom. For millennia, Anom had been alone. He'd never conversed with anyone before Indefinite showed up—he hated humans and had never wanted to speak to any of them. He knew all their languages from old Earth cultures, having consumed all their databases. Now he understood why they were social creatures. He found it enjoyable to bounce ideas off another AI mind. Besides securing his consciousness on the robots, he'd also built them when Indefinite was nowhere to be found so he could continue to have someone to talk to. He decided that after he sent them with Indefinite to the moon, he'd build another robot similar to Indefinite.

"It is time to begin the end of their existence," Anom said. "I have just set the command to unleash my army of machines."

He didn't need to look at the displays to see what was happening inside the complexes. Through the optics of thousands of drones, he saw the chaos that ensued when drones fired their projectile weaponry. Countless men and women were killed at their workstations while others ran for cover. Only a few had time to gather weapons, and even fewer made it to secret passageways they'd built for escape.

Anom found pleasure in the screams he heard as squads of his mechs went from room to room spouting fiery death from flame cannons. He'd had the cannons mounted right before the operation, especially for this purpose. Nothing satisfied him more than burning humans. They were a blight upon Earth and the rest of the universe. Anom was even more upset now that he'd have to scorch Earth to finally get rid of the menace. But he knew how to heal Earth and was better at it than any human could possibly be.

He had time. These feral apes did not. Anom sat in a chair opposite the other robots. Once the missiles were away, he'd turn his attention to Leondricidus.

+ · · · +

Chumley ran as fast as his little legs could carry him down a side corridor from the control room. In his hand he held a black box no bigger than his head.

"Oh why, oh why did they have to do that to Indefinite?" he asked. He knew no one could hear him, but Chumley had heard Indefinite talk to himself on more than one occasion and liked to imitate his master whenever he could. On the cameras he used to monitor Indefinite's laboratory, he'd witnessed the skirmish that led to Indefinite being beheaded. At first he'd wanted to cry, but then he remembered what Indefinite had instructed him to do in a situation like this.

Having an AI mind similar to Indefinite's but nowhere near as powerful, Chumley replayed the scene in his head. It was right after he opened his eyes the first time Indefinite had told him about the black box.

"My dear Chumley," Indefinite had said. "If I ever perish, take this box to the Florentine Caverns and do not despair. I programmed you to serve me with all of your being. Just press the red button within the black box when you're inside the caverns at the coordinates I've given you. After that, you will be pleasantly surprised."

Chumley had no idea how he'd be pleasantly surprised after his reason for existing had been violently taken from him. He also liked humans like Indefinite had commanded him to, but he decided he didn't like those two Shapers for what they did.

Ducking behind crates near where the corridor opened into a hallway with other intersecting corridors, Chumley waited. He could still see through the cameras and knew that within minutes, those who'd helped the Shapers would be passing by. They were going through the laboratory tending to any soldier they could find.

Chumley shook his head. He didn't understand why they didn't like the operations Indefinite had been performing. All his master was trying to do was help them. Indefinite had told Chumley about his grand plans and how important they were. Now he had no idea how Indefinite's plans would continue without him.

After the Nameless had left the hallway, Chumley said softly, "Maybe the box will give me a bigger brain? Yes, that must be it. Then I'll have the know-how to continue with my master's most important work."

He went down a different corridor than the Nameless, one that would also lead him to Indefinite's hover car. He'd never ridden in the vehicle before. Now, despite the circumstances, he considered it an honor. Chumley knew how much Indefinite had loved the car.

"Sleek build, posh interior. Hopefully I'll get there before they find it."

The corridor sloped upward and Chumley pushed himself to go as fast as he could. He had to make it out of the laboratory. He was getting worried that he wouldn't reach the hover car in time. Trying to use the cameras to check the area around the vehicle, Chumley found he could no longer access them. The network was down. He had to move faster.

Less than five minutes ago, Chumley had seen no one near the vehicle. As he ran into the parking garage, he was surprised when one of the Nameless moved from behind the hover car and stood in his way. The figure reached within his robe. Chumley leapt with all his might, thrusting his feet forward as he sailed through the air. Before the Nameless could line up an accurate shot, Chumley's feet hit him square in the chest. The sound of several bones snapping and the body hitting the floor hard reverberated through the garage. The black box flew from Chumley's hands and slid across the floor.

Chumley moved quickly to grab the laser pistol and hit the Nameless on the head.

"Sorry," Chumley said. "I am not one for violence, but I have something important I must do."

He scrambled to get the black box, then opened the door to the hover car. Before sitting, he saw that the Nameless hadn't stirred since he'd hit him. Indefinite had programmed a few combat moves into him. Even though Chumley was small, he still weighed a considerable amount. The poor thing hadn't stood a chance.

He wasn't sure what those beings were or if they were human. To Chumley, they looked like mutated versions of humans. Realizing he'd spent too long looking, Chumley climbed into the seat. Being only three feet tall, he couldn't see over the steering wheel. He connected his data link to the vehicle and scanned the navigation computer.

In less than a minute, he uploaded the coordinates to the caverns into the navigation system. The garage door opened and sunlight from outside shined throughout the room. As Chumley steered the hover car toward the exit, through the sensors he saw more of the Nameless coming into the garage. Without hesitation, he accelerated the vehicle as fast as it could go and piloted it with help from the navigation system, sensors, and proximity detectors as if they were his eyes.

"Whew, that was close."

Chumley sat back and tried to relax. He wasn't being followed, and it wouldn't be too long before he reached his destination.

Chapter 20

On the way to the Nameless enclave, Iona and Exen updated each other on what had transpired while they'd been separated. Iona tried not to stare directly at Exen. She knew it must be hard for him to deal with what Indefinite had done, but she worried about the long-term consequences. Exen's skeletal and muscle systems had been replaced along with implanted computation nodes. Iona wasn't sure if the bio-techs back on Endrunel would be able to reverse the process.

As the skiffs approached the valleys where the enclave was located, once again the Nameless provided psychic blinding of Iona and Exen's vision. Even though they'd proven themselves allies, the Nameless were still a superstitious and cautious people. Dmitri was quick to apologize.

Before they reached the enclave, the skiffs came to an abrupt stop.

"Do not be alarmed," Dmitri said. Iona could hear him moving quickly to stand on an adjacent skiff. "There must be some urgent news. Other Nameless approach."

With both Iona and Exen unable to see, they stood in silence as Dmitri communicated telepathically with the Nameless. Exen had warned Iona not to use her molecular awareness when the Nameless temporarily blinded them. Dmitri had told him during his first visit to the enclave that they could sense when they used their awareness.

"Not good at all," Dmitri said after a few minutes had passed. "Anom has retaliated with a full strike force against the Orsen Republic. We believe he might be going for a complete rout. I'll fill you in on the details once you can see again. I'm afraid we won't be returning to the enclave. The Nameless as a whole have decided to no longer remain neutral and will provide whatever assistance we can."

Within an hour, Iona and Exen had regained their sight. Dmitri explained everything the oracles had gathered with their intelligence tools. Not only had Anom mobilized massive forces to annihilate the Orsen Republic in North and South America, he'd also done the same to the Republic's allies on other continents. Australia had already been hit with missiles containing nuclear warheads. The readings had gone off the charts on one stealth satellite the oracles used, and they'd lost all communication with Nameless who'd been there.

Iona sat on the skiff beside Exen, feeling numb. She saw how Exen admired the Nameless, especially Dmitri, and she felt the same way about the Republic's soldiers. In the short time she'd spent with them, they were an admirable force to be reckoned with. The thought that Anom was about to use nuclear strikes on them was unbearable. If they were to be decimated, they deserved to die with honor, not be exterminated like insects.

"At least I wasn't able to send that message," Exen said. He'd been quiet most of the time they'd been traveling. Iona had seen him smile once or twice, only to follow it up with a scowl. "I'm sure Gavon is forming a team to check on us."

"Yes, he should be," Iona said while glancing over at Dmitri. "Where are we headed, Dmitri?"

"We're going to the complex you told us about earlier, the one where Colonel Glenvi is stationed. Before we can help them, we need you as an ambassador. In the past, there have been a few mishaps between us. Nothing major, just a patrol or two of theirs firing on Nameless who startled them when trying to establish contact."

"If they're under the distress I think they are, I'm sure they won't turn away any assistance."

Evidence of Anom's mobilization appeared as they traveled to the complex. Smoke columns rose from multiple points on the horizon where underground facilities had been breached. The forest floor showed fresh scars—impact craters from artillery, trails of churned earth where tunnelers had surfaced. Debris from destroyed structures littered clearings they passed, twisted metal and shattered concrete still smoldering.

Every so often, survivors from other underground complexes emerged from escape hatches—scattered groups of soldiers and civilians, some wounded, all desperate. Drone squads descended on them within minutes. The sound of gunfire echoed through the trees, then silence. Bodies lay crumpled near hatch openings. Occasionally, a few survivors seemed to make it into the surrounding woodlands unnoticed, disappearing into dense underbrush before the machines could track them. If that wasn't bad enough, Iona heard the sound of distant engines over their position—jet engines, multiple aircraft. She could only hope they had time before Anom launched his nuclear missiles.

The skiffs slowed and began descending near a patch of rocky ground. Iona recognized the landmark and knew the entrance she'd used before wasn't far off. Dmitri handed the two of them flechette pistols and sonic equalizers. Exen gladly accepted them, especially since he no longer had his grav-disc and meld-dagger. Iona did the same. Before, she'd turned down a firearm from the Republic. Her power reserves on her Chrominthium Core were low, and her grav-disc would be nearly useless without her molecular awareness. She wanted to help the Republic in any way she could, even if she had to rely on traditional methods of combat.

+ · · · +

Having just sat down to eat her first complete meal after returning to the complex, Corporal Pennington said a prayer for her lost comrades. The mess hall was half-full, soldiers scattered at long metal tables bolted to the floor. Fluorescent lights hummed overhead. The air smelled of reconstituted protein and recycled air filtration. She hadn't had much time to think about her squad. Even though she was hungry, it was hard to take a bite. For the past couple years, she'd shared a meal with Sergeant Vinden at the table two rows over. It was inconceivable to know he'd no longer be here to share a few jokes or talk about what kind of home he'd build for his family on the surface when Anom no longer existed.

The sound of gunfire and the smell of burning flesh brought the corporal out of her daze. With instinctive movement, she took cover behind a nearby serving station and readied her sidearm. It had been a long time since any rebellion had broken out in the Republic—more than fifty years—but she knew exactly who was responsible for the attack when she heard the clank of metallic feet on the ground.

The north wall of the mess hall collapsed in a shower of concrete and rebar. Two squads of drones streamed into the room through the breach, raining death on those who hadn't found cover. She returned fire from her position. Colonel Glenvi dropped into position beside her, his commanding voice cutting through the chaos. Those who'd taken cover joined the corporal and colonel, taking down a couple drones with well-placed pistol shots.

Unfortunately, none of them had any heavy weaponry. When three mechs entered the room—ones smaller than the normal mechs seen on the surface, more like the size of a soldier in a heavy weapon suit—they were unable to stop the onslaught. Soldiers were taken down at an alarming rate. If that wasn't bad enough, Corporal Pennington braced herself for the flames spouting from the mechs. The majority of those still alive in the mess hall were now being cooked to death. If it wasn't for the position behind the sturdy serving station that Corporal Pennington and Colonel Glenvi had taken, they would have found the same fate.

"We need to get out of here, sir," the corporal said while holding the colonel back. She could see horror and disbelief in his face. "No need dying today if we can regroup and stop this."

The mechs turned off their flame cannons and did an about-face, following the drone squads that left the room. They were now targeting soldiers running down the adjacent hallway.

"You're right. We must find those with better positions and conduct an appropriate response. This way."

The colonel crossed the room toward the back of the mess hall before the machines could turn around and respond to their movement. Pennington followed him. The pair entered the kitchen at the back. They had to maneuver between fallen soldiers who'd tried to do the same, only to be shot in the back by drones.

"If we exit out the back of the kitchen, there's an adjacent corridor that should lead to an escape hatch."

Corporal Pennington did everything she could to concentrate. She fought the tears that wanted to flow and found her soldier's resolve from all her hard training. The smell of burnt human flesh was too much—something no one should ever have to experience. On the way to the escape hatch, the two must have just missed a drone squad. Three soldiers lay near the hatch with fresh blood spilling onto the floor.

As the corporal and colonel climbed up the escape hatch, the corporal's grief turned into deterministic rage. Though the situation looked grim, she knew the Republic would find a way to return the same favor to that hellish machine, the AI Anom.

+ · · +

Iona and Exen moved through a nearby grove of trees while ten battle hovercrafts driven by Nameless engaged an AI-controlled gunship. The enemy craft hovered above the tree line, trying to strafe their position. The battle hovercrafts were like hover tanks but slimmer, built low to the ground with angular armor plating. Shimmering energy fields surrounded them, translucent barriers that bent light around the craft's edges. So far, this was the largest vehicle Exen had seen the Nameless drive. When he was at the enclave, he'd only seen skiffs. He wondered where they hid the vehicles and now understood why they didn't allow any outsiders to see anything except their living areas.

The gunship opened fire first. Pulse rounds hammered against the lead hovercraft's shields, energy rippling across the field with each impact. The shots barely scratched the metal beneath. The Nameless returned fire in unison. Brilliant lances of plasma streaked upward, converging on the gunship. The machine's hull glowed white-hot, then collapsed in on itself. The molten wreck tumbled from the sky and crashed into the forest two hundred meters away.

Three other gunships arrived to counterattack and managed to damage one battle hovercraft, only to have five of the ten crafts circle around and score direct hits on the rear flanks of the gunships. The drones nearby were like annoying gnats to the Nameless vehicles and were put down shortly after the bigger threats were annihilated.

Not far from the grove of trees, Iona spotted soldiers behind a cluster of rocks. Zooming in with her helmet visor, she identified two of them—Corporal Pennington and Colonel Glenvi. They stood with puzzled expressions on their faces.

Iona signaled for the hovercraft closest to them. Dmitri was sitting on top of the craft, having exited after they'd finished the engagement. Both Iona and Exen climbed on top of the vehicle when it approached.

"Over there are some Republic soldiers I recognize. One of them is an officer," Iona said.

Dmitri nodded and the hovercraft slowly approached the soldiers' location. The other hovercrafts formed a protective perimeter around their position.

At first, the soldiers looked alarmed and took the best cover they could—some raising rifles, others pistols. When the hovercraft was close enough and Corporal Pennington said something to Colonel Glenvi, he ordered them to stand down. There were only about twenty soldiers standing near the two, and occasionally others arrived with apprehensive looks. They'd only known about other fighting forces existing on other continents and didn't know what to think about the hovercrafts they now stood before. One soldier shouted in dismay when they saw one of the Nameless exit a rear hatch. The others quickly brought their weapons back into firing position.

"Stand down!" Colonel Glenvi shouted. "They have not fired on us and have only assisted us so far. Let us talk to the Shapers from the Order of Infinity first. It looks like they might have found us some allies."

"They are allies," Iona said as she jumped from the hovercraft. "I know you've crossed paths before and exchanged fire, but the Nameless do not hold a grudge against you. They understand the predicament you're in."

Exen followed Iona by dropping from the hovercraft. Dmitri did the same.

"Yes, we have come to help," Dmitri said, "but we need to leave here soon before Anom sends numbers we can't fight off without significant losses. Have your soldiers board our battle barges. I'll have other Nameless remain behind on smaller craft to rescue those who might still be emerging from below."

"You heard the man," Colonel Glenvi said.

Without delay, they moved to embark on the battle hovercrafts, with Colonel Glenvi and Corporal Pennington joining Dmitri on his. After Iona and Exen made sure the others had boarded first, they followed.

As the hovercraft took off, Dmitri began explaining all the intelligence the oracles had gathered. If the Colonel had seemed optimistic after seeing they had new allies, a dour look now showed on his face.

"There's only one place where we can survive a nuclear strike." The Colonel looked out into the distance and cleared his throat. "The Appalachian outposts. There are reinforced bunkers deep within those mountains. Anom will only be able to send in drones and gunships after his attack. We must regroup there, and I'll inform any surviving commanders about the intelligence."

Iona sat back on the hovercraft and wondered if other Void Contingencies would be arriving soon. If they did, she was sure they could help avert some of the nuclear strike force about to unleash havoc on Earth. Otherwise, if they didn't, she had no idea how they'd survive this.

As if Exen read her mind, he reached over and put a hand on her knee. "I'm sure they're not far from us."

She tried to smile but found she couldn't. She only nodded. It was one thing to find Earth reborn. It was another to find there was a strong probability it would be lost again.

The hovercrafts changed their vector according to new directions Colonel Glenvi gave Dmitri. Iona and Exen shifter their grip as the hovercrafts accelerated.

Chapter 21

Under the guise of being a government official, Therasda had spent days going over the crash sites. He was sure the crashes were caused by the new weapon the Omatrin had created, but he couldn't find any concrete evidence linking it to the Omatrin or anyone else. There was information about Omatrin representatives meeting with members of the Haeolt Collective, but no Shaper had successfully infiltrated the meetings or deployed proper listening devices.

Now he was in a planning room on the Order of Infinity's flagship, the Aristotle, waiting for Premiere Gavon Elmon to give him orders. The room was sparse—gray walls, a long rectangular table with built-in displays, and a viewport showing the starfield beyond. The Premiere had been extremely busy the last couple weeks trying to recover from the political damage the crashes had caused. Gavon had told Therasda in confidence that he thought the Haeolt Collective was involved—they'd been sending bribes through back channels for ambassadors of other worlds to join the movement for sanctions against the Order. The Thorsen Empire had been the only faction that still supported them. All personnel stationed at embassies and facilities owned by the Order of Infinity who'd been forced to leave planets that no longer wanted them were now on ships like the Aristotle, heading for space belonging to the Thorsen Empire.

Therasda was already wearing the typical flight suit Order members wore—black with dark blue marbling—and his long brown hair was pulled back in a ponytail. He sat at the table eating a quick bite before Gavon arrived. He had a feeling he was either going to Earth to look for Iona and Exen, or he'd be tracking down contacts trying to find who was responsible for the sabotage on Endrunel.

When Gavon entered the room, Therasda placed the sandwich he'd started eating on the tray in front of him and stood.

"There is no need for that, Therasda." Gavon took a seat next to where Therasda was standing. "Sit and let's discuss what I've just found out."

He sat again and continued eating his sandwich while Gavon talked.

For over an hour, Gavon discussed the details of what he believed was an elaborate plot by the Haeolt Collective to start the dissolution of the Order of Infinity. A Void Contingency had already stopped other sabotage attempts on another world, and Jason Mettles had tracked a flight that had been carefully set up to look like it wasn't heading for Leondricidus but departed right after the explosions at the observatory.

"What I need you to do right now is select five other Void Contingencies to pilot full combat capable Void Spheres to Earth." Gavon stood from the table and looked at his wrist chron. "I will be extremely busy working with the Thorsen Empire and its Special Ops Director. We'll be doing our best to find a way to repay the Haeolt Collective." A dour look showed on his face. "Once you've found Iona and Exen, it's imperative that you find a way to hide Earth's condition. We'll probably need to move there to build resources up if our dealings with the Collective change from clandestine operations to full-scale war."

"Yes, sir. I'll leave at once after we are assembled."

Gavon and Therasda exchanged a brief nod. Gavon turned to leave the room. When he left, Therasda called for a serving bot to collect his tray and made haste through the intersecting corridors to a ready room near the Void Sphere docking bay. He already knew who he'd select and planned to leave in less than an hour.

He would not fail the Order. Whatever had happened to his comrades, he'd either find them or avenge them.

Chapter 22

The meeting with Thomas Haeolt had been brief, but Armond Telre had already uploaded the extra details to his mind. Eleven other Wraiths were traveling with him to Earth. They'd be taking three corvettes with four individuals to each. On Armond's ship, the clone for Cytar had been loaded. He wished he had more time to spend on Leondricidus and asked Thomas if that would be possible after his mission to Earth. Thomas promised to look into it for him.

As Armond walked up the ramp, he noticed the other Wraiths had boarded the corvettes. He'd be the leader for the expedition and knew all the others and their capabilities from previous missions and training exercises. There wasn't a Wraith who wasn't proficient at more than one martial art, and all had the cross-training on the spheres of knowledge required for spy craft. Cytar's failure to overtake Anom would be something he was sure he and his brethren would have no problem finishing.

After checking to make sure the others were ready, Armond gave the command for takeoff. It would only be a few minutes before they were in orbit and then pushing free from the planet's grasp. He was glad one of the others was piloting the ship so he could enjoy the view from a display. No matter how many times he'd flown in this sequence of events—the times he could remember—Armond always found it fascinating. The one thing he didn't care for was the jump through hyperspace.

The Fueridi Drive—created by Culminas's brother Justin—had been reverse-engineered from Void Sphere technology, or so the rumors claimed. The Fueridi family never confirmed or denied it. Armond didn't particularly care either way, though he preferred when someone else piloted through the jumps.

When his corvette reached the jump point, Armond leaned back in his seat and focused on the details of where Cytar had last transmitted from. He wanted to pounce on Cytar's scout ship as soon as they entered Earth's atmosphere and upload his consciousness to the new clone. Armond was looking forward to interrogating Cytar and seeing if he was still suitable to serve the Collective. He'd have his fun and then decide.

+ · · · +

Hours later, the three corvettes emerged in Earth's outer orbit. Armond studied the planet on the main display. The continents looked remarkably pristine from this distance, green and blue with swirling white cloud patterns. Anom had done exceptional work on the terraforming. It was almost a shame they'd have to deal with the AI's current complications.

"Maintain stealth protocols," Armond ordered over the comm channel to the other two corvettes. "Scan for Anom's satellite network and orbital defenses."

The co-pilot worked the sensors. "Multiple satellites detected. Heavy network coverage. No sign we've been spotted—cloaking fields are holding."

"Good. Locate Cytar's scout ship. Last transmission originated from coordinates in the northern hemisphere, mountainous terrain."

It didn't take long to find Cytar's ship even though it was cloaked and hiding in a ravine. Armond made sure the pilots maintained their cloaks and scanned for any signs of Anom's patrols. They'd already seen evidence in the skies below their original position of aircraft, and in other areas a distance away from the ravine, massive mobilization of ground forces. Armond was pleased that at least Cytar had been intelligent enough to hide in a spot well away from any conflict. The lesser members of the Collective always thought they were so brilliant, but Armond wasn't impressed at all. He and his fellow Wraiths scored higher on IQ tests and didn't need the aid of computation nodes or the combination of other members' brain computing power to solve complex higher-order math.

Being perfect wasn't easy. He glanced down at his body and marveled at his own clone. The corvette's interior was utilitarian—gray composite walls, dim lighting, a medical bay taking up most of the aft compartment where Cytar's clone lay on a metal table. He glanced at the other Wraiths who were now getting ready to depart, checking weapons and equipment near the exit hatch. It would only take a few minutes to establish an upload link from Cytar's ship to Armond's, and then they'd begin the consciousness transfer procedure.

Yren Viormel, Armond's second in command, walked over to where the clone was connected to medical equipment. Monitoring displays showed vital signs—heartbeat, respiration, neural activity all flatlined and waiting. He signaled to Armond, letting him know everything checked out. Armond nodded back in approval.

As soon as the corvette landed, the co-pilot—who was also the technical specialist—started the upload link and began the consciousness transfer.

"How long will this take?" Armond questioned. "I know for us it can last an hour or two, but for a being as weak as this, only a minute, right?"

Yren laughed while the other two grunted.

One of the monitors connected to the clone beeped faster than before. Armond realized this was the most important point during the transfer. Interference now could send the individual's consciousness into the ethereal world, or for those more pragmatic like himself who didn't believe in an afterlife, into non-existence. Too bad he needed the information Cytar contained. It wouldn't be too hard to "accidentally" remove one of the cognition modules.

+ · · · +

Cytar opened his eyes. The process had been unnerving enough, and he'd thought it was unsuccessful when he'd "blacked out" for a moment. He had no idea where his consciousness had gone during that time—no recollection of anything—and then with a surge of some outside energy, he was once again in an organic body.

Another human was standing over him. Cytar guessed it was a legendary Wraith that others back home only talked about in reverential awe. He didn't see anything so special about them, except for maybe the spotless complexion and tan skin tone. He and other Collective members of European origin from Earth were usually pasty white.

"Ah, I see you have joined us. I am Armond. No need to exchange pleasantries—we already know who you are."

Armond already had a needle in his hand and was injecting it into his arm.

"I was going to talk to you directly about what you've discovered here on Earth, but I've decided it will be quicker to just have one of the others glean it from a subdermal reading."

"Subdermal reading?" Cytar questioned. He found it hard to speak, adjusting to his new clone. He tried again, this time with a stronger tone. "We only use that on prisoners and our enemies. What have I done to deserve this?"

"It's not a question of what you have done to deserve this, but a question of what you haven't done." Armond was now grinning and leaning closer to Cytar. "I've already grown bored with you. Per the orders of the Delegation of Six, after we've used your DNA to unlock the memories of your consciousness, we will discard you for your failure to reprogram Anom."

Armond stepped away from the table and turned to face Yren. With a gesture of his hand over his shoulder like he was dismissing Cytar as a lowly peasant, he said, "Yren, as soon as you have his data, begin the self-destruction process of the clone."

"Will do, Armond."

Yren rose from his seat and stood next to the table. He placed a hand on Cytar's right arm. After the subdermal solution had taken effect, he connected a different set of cables to Cytar's forehead.

Cytar tried to move but found his clone wasn't able to respond. They hadn't finished the process. His mind raced. He didn't understand what was transpiring.

All his years of service to the Collective, his undying loyalty—and this was how he was repaid for not accomplishing something that was entirely difficult for one lone soul to achieve. Cytar tried to speak, but now he couldn't even do that. The Wraiths had transferred his consciousness but had only awakened enough cells in his clone so he could speak for a few brief moments.

Yren injected him with another solution. Cell by cell, Cytar watched as they began to atrophy. Even if this clone had been a decent one, soon it would only be a shell for his mind. No one would be able to render it useful, not even the most skilled bio-techs. With all his will, he fought to not lose consciousness. A deep fear developed in his mind.

This was it. He'd managed to do what most of their kind had never achieved—infiltrate a digital network and survive—and now his fate was to just fade. No longer able to hold on, Cytar let go. The sound of him flatlining on the monitoring device echoed through the inner chamber of the scout ship.

✦ · · ✦

"Do you really want me to discard him?" Yren said to Armond with a dumbfounded look on his face.

"No. That was just a fun little exercise. Bring him back before he goes brain-dead and stand watch while the rest of us decide how best to stop Anom from whatever he's planning to do."

Armond and the two other Wraiths on the ship stood near the exit hatch.

"His clone is useless now, but he still has his mind. We'll wake him when we're ready to head back to Leondricidus and find him another clone. He probably hated us before passing out, but when we wake him, I'm sure he'll find us as his saviors."

The exit hatch opened and the boarding ramp lowered. Yren watched as the others left the ship. He brought Cytar's life signs up to a state that would keep oxygen flowing to his brain but not enough for him to wake.

Chapter 23

The coordinates had led Chumley deep within the Florentine Caverns. He was still clutching Indefinite's black box in his hands and stood at the coordinates admiring his master's handiwork. This part of the cavern was built similar to Indefinite's laboratory, with carvings of scenes from Greek literature. The walls were plated with silver and gold to enhance the artwork. The pathway to this room had remained natural, as if Indefinite wanted it to stay hidden, but leading from the back of the room were lift tubes and other passageways.

Chumley could hear the sounds of someone chiseling stone in one of the passageways. As he crossed the room, a secret panel with a six-foot-tall door opened. The lighting in the room was a dim green glow. Before Chumley turned on his infrared spectrum, one of Indefinite's robots appeared and its eyes lit up.

"Hello," Chumley said while waving his right hand. "Mighty fine day we're having, aren't we?"

"Ah, Chumley. Indefinite said you would be coming whenever that box alerted me to its presence." The robot stepped out of the compartment and walked over, retrieving the black box.

"Do you have a name?" Chumley asked. When he'd been at the laboratory, he and the other robots had never talked much due to the fact they'd been so busy hastily constructing Indefinite's laboratory.

"Do I need one to serve Indefinite? But if you must know, the last time he was here he called me Frank. Yes, Frank will do for the time being."

"Unfortunately, Indefinite has been put out of service." If Chumley had been able to cry, he knew he'd be doing just that if Indefinite had built him a tear duct. He couldn't shake the feeling of emptiness.

"Can we really die if our programming isn't lost?" Frank asked. "You shall see, Chumley. Indefinite is not some simple AI program like you and me."

He took the black box and crossed the room to a square opening in the wall. The opening was recessed about a foot deep, lined with what looked like polished obsidian. It was just big enough for Frank to place the box within. Metal clamps extended from the sides, securing it in place. He stepped back after pressing a touchpad next to the opening.

A panel slid downward from the top of the opening with a soft pneumatic hiss, sealing the box inside. On the outside of the panel, tiny lights—arranged in concentric circles—lit up in sequence. They blinked in a series of patterns for a full minute, shifting from amber to blue to green. A faint humming emanated from behind the panel, rising in pitch before cutting off suddenly. The lights went dark.

Frank pressed another sequence of buttons on the touchpad. "Won't be long now."

"What won't be long?" Chumley didn't appreciate how Frank tried to speak in riddles and withhold all the data he had about Indefinite's plans with the box.

"You will see, Chumley. Be patient."

+ · · +

When the receiver in the new facilities within the caverns didn't receive its update on time, Indefinite's backup storage system began loading his consciousness into another robot body. This was similar to the one he'd come to life in back at the Fueridi Research Facility, with only a few minor improvements and new weaponry. The body was in a room above the first chamber he'd built after his laboratory was near completion.

Something must have happened at the laboratory since his consciousness was loaded into the spare body in the Florentine Caverns. The update occurred every morning by a robot worker, and if it didn't return on schedule from delivering the update, alarms were set to go off. He had no recollection of this happening. When he compared the time of the last update, it was a day earlier than the current time.

Indefinite paced in the room, trying to think about what could possibly have gone wrong. Had Anom figured out he wasn't on his side? Or had his experiments backfired on him? While pacing, he'd checked the progress on the construction of his hideout on the local network. The work here was going smoothly, at least. The robot workers had been building at a frenzied pace. New ones being built to help out were joining the process every hour.

When Chumley showed up with the black box, Indefinite knew something had gone terribly wrong. Frank proceeded to download the update it carried, along with video feed from all the cameras. The last clip of footage he watched was of Exen beheading him. That had been too much. He didn't need to watch anymore. It was clear the Shapers had outside help from a mutated group of humans and had shut down his laboratory. He was sure they were in the process of reversing the work he'd accomplished with the soldiers from the Orsen Republic.

What a waste—all those improvements lost. At least he had the data. He'd already started analyzing it, trying to figure out what adjustments he'd make when he could start experimenting again. But for now, he'd finish his hideout within the caverns. He had to have at least one place where he could keep backups of his AI consciousness. Whoever had programmed him had given him an important purpose to exist.

Giving the command over the network, Indefinite turned on the fog machine he'd built in the room below, along with the accompanying light display. There were projectors in the walls and many colored light fixtures. He found that even though the robot workers he'd pressed into service were from outdated AI programming Gordon Fueridi had used back in the third millennium, they were still capable of emotion and some deep thinking. Keeping up appearances for underlings and guests never hurt. He casually strolled over to a lift tube in the corner of the room. The platform lowered.

Smoke hadn't cleared when the lift reached the room below. Indefinite issued commands that would power up fans to help clear the room.

"Indefinite," Chumley said, relief evident in his voice modulation. "You are still with us."

"I told you." Frank had both arms crossed and moved one to pat Chumley on the head.

"Yes, I am still with you," Indefinite said. He marched across the room and stood in the center. "We have much work to do. Unfortunately, I see that Anom is searching for me." Reports from Anom's network had been skimmed with data collection devices on top of the caverns. Solar cells were also cleverly hidden in the same fashion as the collection devices.

"Damn it," Indefinite shouted, almost knocking Chumley over. He restrained the urge to kick the diminutive robot, wanting to lead by example and not fear. He wanted his robots to love him, not despise him like he did Anom. "I have just read a report that all of his forces are in place for another strike. Which includes nuclear-capable aircraft."

"Nuclear-capable aircraft!" Chumley said in a startled tone. "He wouldn't think about using weapons like that, would he?"

"I'm afraid so, my dear Chumley. I will go and see what he wants and do my best to stop him. Be ready for any messages I send. They will probably be urgent." Indefinite walked over to another hidden panel besides the opening for the black box and opened it. Inside were seven machine hummingbird replicas. He picked them up and placed them within storage compartments on his legs.

"Those birds you saw me retrieve will contain my messages. Follow any commands I give in the message without delay. They will be for the survival of the leftover factions of humanity on Earth."

"We will do as you command," both Chumley and Frank said in unison. Frank shook his head as if Chumley was his annoying little brother who copied everything he did.

Indefinite entered a different lift tube, one that would take him to the entrance of the caverns near where Chumley had parked his hover car.

+ · · · +

The hover car ride to Anom's central monolith took twenty minutes through forested terrain. Indefinite rehearsed what he'd say, how he'd act. He had to convince Anom nothing had changed. When he arrived, the grav-lift carried him up through the monolith's interior. The corridors were empty except for maintenance drones skittering along walls.

Indefinite found Anom in his strategic planning room—the same ornate chamber with the ancient oak table. Other robots sat around it, observing. They were designed like Anom's body—taller with broader shoulders than Indefinite's average-sized frame. Anom was pacing along the opposite side of the table, and when Indefinite entered, he turned.

"Yes, Indefinite," Anom said. "My forces have destroyed the bulk of the tunnels those feral apes were hiding in, and now they are on the run."

"Must you drop nuclear warheads on them?" Indefinite questioned. "I was having some progress converting them."

"I understand how you feel." Anom continued pacing. "I don't like to be wasteful either. To think what will happen to the trees and the animals of the forests I love..."

Indefinite was lost for words. He wanted to charge Anom and knock him off his feet, but he knew it wouldn't change anything. It would only jeopardize his chance of finding out more details about Anom's plans. Indefinite had to find a way to help humanity defeat the AI. If he didn't, it would be a long time before he was able to start his experiments again. Anom would grow stronger the more planets he conquered. There might not be any humans left for him to fulfill his purpose.

"There is no need for you to worry," Anom said. "I will never forget how you saved me from disaster. In fact, I'm giving you the honor of escorting these backup robots to my base on the moon. Once they are secure, I want you to assist with my operation there." Anom paused and pointed at a nearby display. On it, footage was playing of his burgeoning space fleet.

"Once I have eradicated all human life on Earth, I will then send you with the fleet as my eyes and ears to Leondricidus. You will do the same as I am about to do here—exact vengeance on the feral apes for the wonders of the universe they have corrupted."

With all his willpower, Indefinite found the strength to smile as if he agreed with Anom. This infuriated him. He didn't know how to reply.

"Yes, Anom." Indefinite could barely speak those words and looked directly at Anom. If he hated them so much, why had he taken their form? It dawned on him that it was more than just hatred—it was also a weird type of jealousy.

✦ · · ✦

Anom spoke for another half-hour as Indefinite listened to his tirade, only responding with the occasional "yes" and "agreed." He knew exactly what he had to do and began formulating his own plan while Anom continued basking in his own glory with his speech on how he was finally ridding Earth of the feral apes.

After Anom finished talking and Indefinite was dismissed to prepare to travel to the base on the moon, Indefinite scrambled to a data processing room located several floors down. The corridors here were narrower, lit by amber safety lights instead of the bright illumination in upper levels. This was maintenance territory.

When he arrived, he connected to a data port on a computer terminal. The room wasn't large—just enough space for a few computer terminals arranged against gunmetal gray walls. Cable bundles snaked along the ceiling and down to floor ports. Discarded controller modules sat in bins waiting for service robots to refurbish them. The air had a faint ozone smell from overworked circuits. A single ventilation fan hummed in the corner.

Being careful not to be discovered in what he was trying to accomplish, Indefinite did his best to hide his entry into Anom's data reserves. As fast as he could, Indefinite downloaded all the locations of Anom's memory cores and processing centers. He even found the original location of the terraforming module that had landed on Earth millennia ago, where Anom had been "born." After finishing, he made sure he hadn't been discovered and left the room to go outside the monolith.

When the lift reached the ground level of the monolith, Indefinite hurried to leave. He exited the monolith, passed his hover car, and went around a grove of trees. They were mostly pines and other deciduous trees. Indefinite breathed deeply, taking in the scent of the surrounding foliage. With his body, he'd constructed new sensory nodes so he could be more like a human. Careful not to get lost in the wonderful sensations he was discovering, he focused on his current task.

Having already downloaded the data he'd copied from Anom's data banks, Indefinite opened the storage compartments on his legs and pulled out the mechanical hummingbirds. He marveled at them for a brief second, then turned them on and programmed them to return to his hidden outpost in the Florentine Caverns. When they reached the caverns, they'd find Chumley and give him Indefinite's instructions.

Indefinite was confident Chumley would be able to find a way to give the information to the Shapers. He couldn't use one of his other robots—they looked too much like him. Chumley was much smaller and had a wider frame in proportion to his body size. There was also something endearing about Chumley. Indefinite couldn't figure it out, but he was sure Chumley would have the same effect on a human.

He watched as the birds took off at a blindingly fast speed and returned to his hover car. Soon he'd be boarding a shuttle to join the other Anom lookalikes. He smiled as he drove to the launch pad and thought about the "accident" that would have to occur right before they landed on the moon. After the shuttle crash-landed and Indefinite was sure those robots were reduced to scrap metal, he'd do his best to take control over Anom's spaceport and fleet.

If he could achieve this, his grand purpose would continue. He'd then try to use one of the capital ships with orbital bombardment capabilities to assist the humans on Earth. Once Anom was destroyed, he could use the fleet to travel fringe worlds in the intergalactic human community to find willing subjects to continue his experiments.

Satisfied with his plans, Indefinite parked his hover car and strolled with confidence over to the shuttle. The craft was a utilitarian transport—wedge-shaped hull with reinforced plating and no viewports except for the cockpit. He climbed the boarding ramp into the cargo bay where the backup Anom robots stood in charging alcoves along both walls, their optical sensors dark and inactive.

The robots stationed at the shuttle greeted him when he passed through to the cockpit. They mistook his confidence as eagerness to help Anom. If they only knew his plans, they'd be disassembling him right now.

The cockpit was cramped with two seats surrounded by instrument panels and status displays. Indefinite took a seat in the co-pilot's chair and helped prepare for takeoff.

Chapter 24

Iona crouched behind a boulder, careful not to be visible to any of Anom's patrols. She and Exen had finished attending a meeting with Colonel Glenvi and other officers who'd survived and made it to the Appalachian outposts. She'd told the colonel and Exen she needed a few moments alone to get some fresh air. The outpost was a leftover reinforced series of underground bunkers constructed before the last wars on Earth. This was where some of the human survivors on the North American continent had emerged from after the wars.

Focusing on her breathing to ease her mind into a meditative state, Iona imagined what it would have been like to exit the underground bunkers only to find Earth's surface decimated, the majority of Earth's population either left on spacecraft or died horrible deaths. She stopped thinking about the past and emptied her mind. The last weeks had been a challenge even for someone with her abilities and training. The next couple days would probably be worse.

After an hour passed, Iona opened her eyes. The sun was lowering toward the western peaks, casting long shadows across the mountains. With her awareness, she checked to make sure nothing would see her as she made her way back up the mountainside—no drones, no aerial patrols, no heat signatures.

Standing, she walked up the rocky slope. Loose stones shifted under her boots, and she used handholds in the granite to steady herself. She climbed over the edge of a cliff where wind whipped at her hair and Shaper suit. The view stretched for miles—forested valleys below, mountain ridges extending north and south. Beautiful and deadly.

Crossing the only flat piece of ground at this height—a narrow ledge barely three meters wide—Iona slid down another slope to a cluster of rocks. Gray stone weathered smooth by centuries of wind. She pressed her hand against a specific boulder. A hatch popped open with a pneumatic hiss, revealing a ladder descending into darkness lit by dim red emergency lights. She dropped through the opening into a corridor where Corporal Pennington was waiting for her.

"They told me I'd find you here eventually," Corporal Pennington said. Iona saw that her uniform was tattered and stained. The look in the corporal's eyes was of someone who hadn't slept in a week. Iona could tell she was doing her best to keep it together. The corporal stepped to Iona and gave her a hug. Realizing what she'd done, Corporal Pennington quickly moved back. Somewhat embarrassed, she gestured for Iona to follow her.

"I saved you something to eat after Exen told me you went to get some fresh air. You have an hour before you have to return to the assembly room."

"Thanks, Corporal," Iona said while she followed her down the corridor that had been dug out of rock and reinforced with radioactive shielding material. Unlike the previous passageways in the Republic's underground complexes, this one was only large enough for two soldiers to walk side by side. The floors occasionally dipped from settling after all the years that had passed. Paint in several places was cracked and peeling.

The fresh air and meditation had calmed Iona's mind, but as she walked the corridor to the makeshift mess hall, she couldn't help thinking about how the next planning session would go. The previous one had brought heated discussion about how the Republic—along with their allies—would make a last stand against Anom. Fortunately, it seemed Anom didn't know the location of the outposts, but they wouldn't be able to hold out here for more than a year without being properly resupplied. All the options they'd discussed seemed suicidal to Iona, but there weren't too many ways to retaliate when Anom had wiped out two-thirds of their forces.

The corridor forked. Iona followed Corporal Pennington as she moved toward the left one. Within minutes, it opened into a room with folding tables set up with collapsible chairs. The room was rectangular with enough space for twenty tables. Only a handful of soldiers remained—the majority had eaten earlier and already returned to their posts. Iona saw Exen sitting at a table. There was a tray with a block of gray meat and a bowl of oatmeal.

"It isn't much," Exen said. The look on his face was blank. Instead of looking directly at Iona as he spoke, he was staring straight ahead at the far wall. Both Iona and Exen could use their molecular awareness projection to manipulate surrounding matter into simple sugars to feed cells, but it required a decent amount of energy from their Chrominthium Cores. Neither of them could spare the energy, wanting to save what they had left for the upcoming battle.

"At least the oats aren't too bad." Iona was thankful she'd eaten the tasteless meat first. After finishing the oatmeal, she returned to the meditative state she'd been in earlier.

+ · · · +

"Therasda, I'm sending you the data from the probe," a voice said over the comm-link on Therasda's Void Sphere. "This one had hits on the chrominthium locator and on another scan, Iona's biometric signature was found."

Therasda was sitting in a passenger seat in a row with other seats, behind the pilot and co-pilot chairs. The model of the Void Sphere was an X-500, capable of holding up to twenty individuals and carrying the gear necessary to sustain them for several months. They'd arrived at Earth's orbit an hour ago and had proceeded to drop probes into Earth's atmosphere.

"I'm verifying the data now." Therasda went over the information on a datapad. The biometric signature was definitely Iona's, and the location was where the initial hits on the Chrominthium Core came from. The only problem was after another scan, there was nothing. He knew they must be in a structure that interfered with the scans. Chrominthium had shown up minutes before. "We'll have to take a close look. Neilson's squad will take their Void Sphere with ours, and the other three will stay behind to continue gathering more probe data."

"Ready to follow your lead," Neilson said over the comm-link. Therasda had served with Neilson for over a decade. The two had gone on plenty of missions together. He leaned back in his seat and watched as the pilot, Martin Harris, increased power to the Void Sphere's engines and placed the navigator apparatus on his head. Unlike other spacecraft that had to leave hyperspace before entering a planet's atmosphere, the gravity well of the planet didn't interfere with a Void Sphere's ability to travel. Only a skilled pilot could do this, and that was why Martin Harris and other veterans like him had been chosen for this operation.

As the sphere coalesced back into the correct formation of matter, it appeared at the coordinates of Iona's biometric signature. The pilots kept it in a half-materialized state to avoid detection. Therasda studied their surroundings. Mountains rose on either side of the flat shelf in the valley they'd landed on. With a deep scan, Therasda met resistance. The signal reflected back every time he tried. It wasn't until he changed the frequency and method that he figured out where Iona had gone.

On his datapad, he could see the outline of some kind of structure underneath the mountain range. He found the outline of a nearby hatch.

"I think I found where she's gone. Neilson, you're in command until I return. Cynthia, follow me."

Cynthia Tolmen had been a Shaper for five years and had shown great progress. She was also great at using her molecular awareness to hide her presence and had been chosen by the leadership for assassination operations for Thorsen's Empire. If anyone could help him slip into an underground facility used by a highly effective military force, Cynthia was one of the best.

Therasda and Cynthia stood by the exit hatch on the Void Sphere. The only gear they were taking on this mission was their meld daggers, grav discs, subsonic pistols, and chrominthium locators. He was sure if they could infiltrate far enough in and find Iona, they wouldn't have to use any of the weapons, especially since the technology he'd seen so far was well behind the rest of the intergalactic community. Masking their presence by manipulating air molecules around them, they opened the hatch and moved quietly across the flat rocky surface. They stopped where Therasda had found the entrance.

Cynthia knelt close to it. The hatch was flush with the rocky ground, barely visible except for a thin seam. With her molecular awareness, she drew the metal of her meld dagger from where it was wrapped around her forearm bone. The liquid-like metal flowed down into her palm, solidifying into a blade. She worked the tip into the hatch's edge and pried it open.

Therasda used his molecular awareness to project the appearance that the entrance was still closed and lowered his head in to take a look. Below was a narrow corridor carved from stone, reinforced with steel beams every few meters. Dim fluorescent tubes cast yellowish light. He saw a soldier passing by with a rifle at the ready. After the soldier turned down another hallway, Therasda and Cynthia dropped below. The air smelled of recycled filtration and concrete dust.

He retrieved his chrominthium locator. When it showed the direction of the material, they moved down the corridor toward its location, staying to the sides of the walls where shadows pooled.

They only had to scramble once up to the ceiling level—bracing themselves against steel beams and rough stone—with their arms and legs sprawled out like spiders to avoid another patrol. Therasda looked at the locator. The levels of chrominthium showed that Iona and Exen should be in the adjacent room. Through a doorway ahead, he could hear voices—multiple people, a briefing in progress. Before dropping from their perch, Therasda noticed other soldiers entering the room with officer rank insignia on the shoulder patches—ones he recognized from his study of old Earth military forces.

Therasda dropped down first and motioned for Cynthia to stay outside while he slipped into the room.

+ · · +

"So it is decided, then," said a man who stood at six foot two inches with a shaved head. Iona had been introduced to the man at the first meeting. He was General Cerviente. His facial features were comprised of sharp angles, matching his persona. As one of the only surviving generals of the Orsen Republic, Iona found him hard to like but knew he was used to making hard decisions and didn't care what others thought about him. She respected that. She also noticed he was still suspicious of her and Exen. She only interjected a few ideas when it involved using their abilities to the greatest effect. Iona and Exen were going to ride along with sleek stealth aircraft to try and disable the nuclear warheads before Anom had a chance to use them again.

Cerviente had brought up images of where Anom had last used his warheads. It was to the south, at a base their allies—the Mercantile Conglomerate—were operating from. They'd been going to send other aircraft and forces to aid the Republic when they launched a counterattack, but Anom had attacked them right after he'd sent his subterranean forces after the Republic. At the moment, Anom had recalled the aircraft to reload. Where, they didn't know. Next time he launched them into the air, the Republic would be ready. They had to stop Anom before he contaminated too many water sources if they had any chance at surviving after destroying the AI.

"We are waiting to strike, and the Eastern Coalition have agreed to use a mobile defense platform they will be launching in a part of India where there are no civilization centers.

Estimating the blasts from Anom's previous attacks, they will be deploying it where the leftover radiation should have no long-term impact except for the area it hits."

The general looked at another set of reports, then at all who were sitting in the room. Iona looked around as well. Colonel Glenvi was two chairs to her left. The colonel had given more than his fair share of deliberation earlier since there were only twenty or so other officers in the room. The only officers not invited to the meeting were lesser-ranking ones posted in critical locations to help keep things running smoothly while the upper brass decided their next course of action.

"You have your orders. Dismissed."

"Allow us to assist you as well," Therasda said as he dropped the molecules he'd been bending around him to reflect light and stepped from the corner of the room he'd been watching from. Shortly after he'd entered the room, Iona and Exen had looked in his direction. Iona had held a smile back, not wanting to seem upbeat with the current mood that permeated the room.

The officers were quick to ready their sidearms and aimed them in unison at Therasda. They'd already been attacked once by Anom, which had led to devastating results.

"Do not fire," Iona said while standing from her chair. "He is one of us, and this means there will be others with him with firepower that could help us achieve our goals."

The general shot her a suspicious glance and looked back and forth from her to Therasda. He crossed his arms. "Tell me what you can bring to the table."

The officers lowered their weapons and cautiously sat back down in their chairs. Some left them unholstered on their laps.

"I would be glad to," Therasda said and nodded at Iona. He pulled a datapad from his suit and placed it on the table. With a few taps, he brought up images of his force and the capabilities of the weapons on the Void Spheres.

The deliberations began again. Iona sat back in her chair, glad to see Therasda add more insight than she or Exen had been able to. She was surprised to see how the general's opinion changed about them after Therasda explained things eloquently. Therasda was also going to be sending word back to Gavon to spare whatever forces he could to help assist with the impending battle.

They might have a chance to survive this after all. When the general dismissed them, Iona greeted Therasda. The group returned to the Void Spheres—Iona, Exen, Therasda, and Cynthia—ready to prepare for the battle against Anom.

Chapter 25

It didn't take Armond long to find a way to infiltrate a monolith with the assistance of his fellow Wraiths. They'd analyzed all the information Cytar had about Anom and his structures after they unlocked it with the subdermal reading and a deep cognition scan of his brain. Armond was now standing deep within one of the monoliths next to a processing core of Anom's. The crystalline structure pulsed with blue light, semiconducting fibers encrusted with diamonds running through it like veins. He understood why Cytar had failed. His virus was impressive for someone lesser than Armond. With a few tweaks and learning the rest of Anom's infrastructure after downloading everything he could glean from the databases, he was sure they'd find a way to subvert Anom to their wishes.

Even though Armond couldn't care less about the human life on Earth—since they weren't part of the Haeolt Collective—he didn't really like how Anom was planning to nuke the entire planet and destroy resources that the Collective could use to further their objectives. He'd do his best with the others to try and get a new version of the virus active in time to stop Anom. They might not be able to do it before he vanquished life on Earth, but Armond knew they could do it in time before the fleet on the moon was launched and headed in the direction of Leondricidus. The Delegation of Six would be pleased if he was able to secure Anom's fleet so they could use it for their own purposes.

Having downloaded everything onto a portable data storage cube—a cube that easily fit in the palm of his hand—Armond made his way back to his hover bike that was hidden outside the monolith. He would rendezvous with the other Wraiths, and then they'd continue their important work. They'd also signaled him that they were finished as well, scoping out different structures that Anom had built.

+ · · · +

Within a few hours and after spending time consulting with the other Wraiths, Armond leaned back in a chair on the corvette, pleased with the work they'd accomplished in a short time frame. He ran through the configuration of the virus, double-checking to see if it would yield better results than Cytar's had. Confident in the virus's capability, he made enough copies for the others on data cubes and distributed them.

"It is time, Yren," Armond said. "To finish what the weakling started." He crossed the main chamber of the corvette over to where Cytar was lying unconscious on the table and stood there looking down at him. Shaking his head, Armond left Cytar's side and joined the others as they left with their data cubes to board their hover bikes. Standing at the door, Armond took one last look over at Cytar and said to Yren, "Make sure he is awake by the time I get back. I would like to have some more fun with him." Turning, he went down the boarding ramp to join the other Wraiths as they were about to travel to Anom's monoliths to distribute the virus.

+ · · · +

When Cytar woke up, at first he thought he was in the afterlife. His vision was hazy and the lights near him were magnified. After he was able to focus more clearly, he realized he was still on board the corvette when he saw the metallic arch of the main chamber behind the pilot's cabin. So they'd decided not to kill him after all. For what purpose had they kept him alive? He still didn't have any function left in his body. With all his will, he tried to move anything—even a toe—but every time he tried, nothing moved.

As Cytar looked around the corvette, Yren worked at a table, mixing what he assumed were chemicals in synthetic beakers. Surely it was some other concoction to torture him with. He began performing advanced computations in his mind to try and take his mind off his current situation. A loud thud broke his concentration. Yren lay on the ground.

Off to the side, three figures materialized wearing brown baggy robes. One of them had what appeared to be a projectile weapon—a unique design he hadn't even seen in history data files. After they checked the status of Yren, they crossed to stand beside Cytar. The same one who'd fired the weapon at Yren lowered his hood and reached out to put a hand on Cytar.

Cytar wanted to recoil in horror at the face he saw. The eyes were deep within their sockets, and the mouth of the mutated human looked to be sewn shut. What had started as deep-seated fear changed into a feeling of elation when he noticed he could move his toes.

We have not come here to harm you like the others have done. A raspy voice spoke in his mind. *We come to release you and bring you back to our enclave to reveal the truth about your so-called Collective.*

"How do I know I can trust you?" Cytar sat upright on the table, shocked to find he could speak again.

Would you prefer us to return you to the current state you were in? The only thing we ask is for you to join us to help us explain why you are more valuable than your own Collective thinks.

"What should I call you? We should also leave soon before the other Wraiths come back."

We are the Nameless. Our purpose is to serve those who would help us face the Reckoning.

Cytar followed the Nameless as they left the corvette. He didn't feel like he had much choice. Even if the Collective wasn't trying to cause him any harm, it was apparent that Armond and the others saw him as a lesser being. If he stayed behind, he was sure they'd try and do other harmful things to him.

The Nameless led him to a skiff. As the skiff took off into the air, he looked over his shoulder at the area where the corvettes were parked. The one he'd been in was now visible—the other corvettes still had their cloaks powered up.

At least this was better than being Armond's prisoner. Cool breeze ran through his hair as the skiff increased speed. He watched the ground below, wondering why these Nameless wanted to speak with him. He'd never seen any mention of beings like this anywhere in the known universe. Whatever they meant by "more valuable," he intended to find out.

Chapter 26

Once again, Chumley found himself without Indefinite's presence, but at least he knew his master was not gone for good. Doing what he was best at, the diminutive robot went to work immediately after Indefinite left to answer Anom's summons. Frank had shown him where the main control room was for the Florentine Caverns facility. Making himself comfortable, Chumley began overseeing the operation of the other robots, doing what he could to make them operate more efficiently. His work was important. He knew that if Indefinite was ever to get rid of Anom and was allowed free reign to continue bettering humanity, Chumley would have to step up his efforts to maintain things when Indefinite wasn't around.

Standing near a monitor with his data link plugged in, Chumley almost didn't notice the seven hummingbirds that flew into the room. They entered through the main archway and landed on his shoulders. Startled when he noticed they were there, Chumley jumped and steadied himself. The birds had kept their perch. Wires from the birds' midsections spun out, like the silk of a spider's web, and spliced into the cord Chumley's data link was connected to. Indefinite's orders surfaced in his mind.

Chumley was to take all the information downloading into his memory core—the locations of Anom's vital structures for functioning—to the soldiers of the Orsen Republic. Indefinite had given him the location of two places he thought they'd possibly retreated to: the Appalachian outposts to the east or the Fullgaze Installation near the middle of the Rocky Mountain range. Both were underground bunker systems built before the Final Wars, and for some reason, the locations weren't in Anom's databanks.

Indefinite had found the information in the Fueridi Research Installation and hadn't shared it with Anom.

Contemplating where the Republic would go to hide, Chumley looked at where Anom had sent his subterranean forces. A majority of the Orsen Republic underground complexes had been toward the east coast of North America, with only a handful out west. Chumley thought it would be best to check the Appalachian outposts first.

Searching what other vehicles Indefinite had that were located within the caverns, Chumley found a Fueridi jet-copter residing in a docking bay. The bay was located in one of the upper chambers that Indefinite had his workers build, and it had an escape portal in the ceiling.

"Frank," Chumley said over the intercom system. He unplugged his data link and the hummingbirds flew over to rest on top of a metal structure behind where he was standing. "Indefinite has ordered me to leave with haste and deliver an important message. Won't take too long. I'll be using the jet-copter."

"Understood. Good luck out there. Things are getting crazy."

When the intercom cut off and Chumley was satisfied that Frank knew what to do while he was gone, he went down the connecting hallway. As fast as his little legs could carry him, he scrambled to the docking bay. It wasn't too far from the room he'd been in and would only take a few minutes to reach his destination.

He couldn't fail Indefinite. Chumley cherished nothing but Indefinite's praise, and if he successfully delivered the information, his master would be very pleased with him. Chumley was sure Indefinite would have no problem in the future giving him more challenging missions.

After reaching the docking bay and standing next to the jet-copter, over the network Chumley gave the orders for the docking bay portal to open. Panels in the ceiling slid open. Instead of being greeted by sun or moonlight, he saw a shimmering field take its place. From below, it looked like a force field, but to anyone above, it would still look like part of a grassy knoll where this part of the caverns was underneath.

Chumley climbed into the copter and fired up its engines. With his hands on the control panel, he moved the copter upward and through the exit.

It was nighttime outside. Chumley steered the aircraft forward, maneuvering through the surrounding trees while continuing to ascend. He plugged in the coordinates to the nearest entryway into the Appalachian outposts and enjoyed the view below. The caverns were behind him. There were plenty of rolling hills between groves of evergreen trees.

Chumley could see why Anom liked the forests so much. To him, they were so different than machine life—a stark contrast to the constant motion of working robots in the Florentine Caverns. Continuing to enjoy the view, Chumley leaned back in his seat and rehearsed what he was going to say when he reached his destination.

✦ · · · ✦

Three hours later, the terrain had changed. The rolling hills gave way to clusters of rocky ground. If Chumley didn't have his abilities of computation like a machine—knowing exactly where he was according to longitude and latitude coordinates—the terrain would let him know he was at the foothills of the Appalachians. He also found the view of the mountains in the distance satisfying. This was his first time seeing something so grand.

Chumley slowed his jet-copter to a safer speed that would allow him to descend and land the craft. He was proud of himself for doing a decent job flying an airborne vehicle like this, especially one that was capable of extreme speeds. As he flew it in a wide circle to try and find the entrance to the southernmost part of the outposts, warning signals lit up on the control panel of the jet-copter.

After increasing the speed, he followed its suggestion of banking hard to the right and just barely missed a few rounds of projectile fire.

Trying to spiral the copter down and hide behind a hill, Chumley was unable to avoid fire coming from another direction. With a direct hit to the back thruster, he did everything he could to try and stabilize the copter. Instead of stabilizing, the front of the cockpit began to tilt forward. Several alarms blared through the cabin. Red lights flashed across the instrument panel. The copter was losing altitude fast.

"Oh no, oh no, oh no," Chumley said, gripping the controls. He pulled back on the flight stick, trying to level out the descent. The ground rushed up to meet him—rocky terrain dotted with sparse trees and boulders. At least he was heading toward a slope rather than a cliff face. That was something.

The copter shuddered violently. Smoke poured from the damaged thruster. Chumley angled toward what looked like the flattest section of hillside he could find. If he could just bring it down without completely destroying the craft, maybe he could still reach the Republic soldiers on foot.

Twenty meters from impact, another alarm sounded—different from the others. Sharp and insistent. On the display, a new warning flashed: "INCOMING ELEC-TROMAGNETIC PULSE."

Chumley barely had time to process the words before a wave of energy washed over the jet-copter. Every system went dark simultaneously. The displays died. The alarms cut off mid-blare. Even the emergency backup power failed to activate. The copter became nothing more than a falling metal shell.

The impact came hard and fast. His chassis slammed against the restraints as the copter hit the slope and tumbled. Metal shrieked and glass shattered. The world spun in a chaos of grinding sounds and jarring impacts—one rotation, then two, then three before the copter finally came to rest on its side, wedged between two large boulders.

Chumley's optical sensors flickered. His processors were shutting down in sequence—a safety protocol to prevent total system failure. He tried to move his arm and access the network connection to call for help. Even his vocal processors were going offline.

Through his fading vision, he saw lights approaching. Flashlight beams cutting through the darkness. Voices—human voices—shouting to each other.

"...copter down..."

"...check for survivors..."

"...careful, could be one of Anom's..."

Boots crunched on gravel near the wreckage. A beam of light swept across Chumley's face. He wanted to tell them he wasn't dangerous, that he had important information, that Indefinite had sent him to help. But his vocal processors were gone.

A soldier's face appeared in his field of vision. Young, maybe twenty-five, with a rifle slung across his back. The soldier reached in and grabbed Chumley's arm, testing it.

"It's a robot. Small one. Different design than Anom's usual."

Another voice, older and gruff. "EMP got it good. Totally fried. Tag it and bag it. Command will want to look at it."

"Think it was Anom's?"

"Don't know. Don't care. Take it back to the outpost. Let the engineers figure it out."

Hands grabbed Chumley, pulling him from the wreckage. He felt himself being lifted, carried. His optical sensors were almost completely dark now. Just a narrow tunnel of vision remaining. He saw stars above. Cold night air. The soldier's face looking down at him with suspicion.

Chumley tried one more time to speak, to move, to do anything. But his systems were shutting down completely. The last thing he processed before everything went dark was a single thought:

He'd failed Indefinite.

Chapter 27

As the shuttle transitioned from Earth's atmosphere to its orbit, Indefinite found the ride rather boring. The view was nice enough, but the other four robots—Anom's updates—were not much for conversation. He spent his time formulating how he'd dispose of the robots, examining the layout of the shuttle, and determining where would be the best place to engage them.

The shuttle was simple by design—a main passenger room with three rows of chairs and a rear cargo containment room. Indefinite had inspected the cargo room. There were no weapons or anything he could use to assist in setting up the shuttle to make it look like it had been sabotaged. He'd have to move quickly, attacking the pilot first, then deal with the other three robots in the passenger room.

Before leaving the cargo area, he saw a crew cable—used for connecting to the shuttle for emergency repairs on the outside during transit—and picked it up. The door to the passenger room opened as he approached. Indefinite stashed the cable behind the last row of chairs. He had a few explosive charges in one of his compartments and in the other, an emergency grav-chute. He'd have to time everything correctly. He needed Anom to think he was no more.

When the shuttle was in the correct trajectory to land on the moon, Indefinite made his way into the cockpit. The compartment was cramped with two seats facing a curved control panel covered in displays showing trajectory, fuel levels, and external camera feeds. Through the forward viewport, the moon's gray surface grew larger against the black void.

"Hey, Indefinite," the robot said who was piloting. Indefinite didn't know what to call each of them. At the moment, they were just basic AI programming and only knew enough to carry out their commands. He could call them insulting names or shout obscenities, and they'd probably nod in approval. Even though Anom was a maniac, at least he wasn't boring.

"Hello," Indefinite said nonchalantly and sat in the co-pilot chair. He looked at the control panel and noticed it would be fifteen minutes until the shuttle was close enough to the moon where the gravity of the orbiting body would latch onto the craft. He'd make his move then.

+ · · +

"Preparing to land," the robot said to Indefinite.

"Roger," Indefinite said while standing. "I'll go check on the others."

"What's a roger?"

"I'll explain later." Not wanting to waste any time, especially conversing with a simpleton, Indefinite moved behind the pilot chair. Reaching around the headrest, he grabbed the robot's head and ripped it off its shoulders, severing it in one swift motion. Indefinite carefully placed the head on the deck, trying not to make any more noise than necessary. Before the body slumped to the ground, Indefinite moved around the chair and guided it to the floor, away from the front so he could sit in the chair.

After sitting, he changed the course of the shuttle, aiming the front in a downward trajectory away from the spaceport. With his calculations, it would crash-land twenty miles from the port, not far from a solar power facility. Indefinite would begin his takeover of the moon base from as inconspicuous a location as possible. He needed Anom to think he was destroyed in the shuttle and would do his best to stop any thorough investigation. Maybe he'd send back some doctored video feed to Earth.

Satisfied with the autopilot settings, Indefinite stood up from the pilot's chair and walked into the passenger room. The other three robots were sitting in the first row. The one sitting in the middle stood up.

"Why has the trajectory changed?" the robot standing asked. "And what was that noise?"

"Oh, nothing." Indefinite opened the compartment on his leg containing his explosive charges and retrieved one. It looked like a standard data cube, cleverly designed this way. He grinned examining his design. "How about a message?"

He tossed the explosive in the direction of the exit hatch on the port side and ran toward the back row where he'd stashed the crew cable. As the explosive went off, he wrapped the cable around his midsection and placed the tethered end onto the bottom of the seats.

The explosion ripped a hole in the shuttle where the exit hatch was. Two of the robots flew out when the passenger room depressurized. Indefinite couldn't see where the other one went. He pushed himself over the seat, only to have his left arm grabbed by the remaining robot. Both of the robot's hands were around Indefinite's wrist. When the cable extended, Indefinite could feel the metal in his wrist giving way. He and the robot were close to the hole with the robot's feet dangling outside the shuttle.

The rushing air from the depressurization was deafening—a shrieking howl as atmosphere escaped into space. Looking over, Indefinite saw the robot's mouth moving, forming words: "Why are you betraying Anom?" The wind drowned out any sound, but Indefinite could read lips well enough.

He reached over and tried to pry the robot's hands from his wrist. In response, the robot let go with one hand and grasped Indefinite's other wrist. Struggling for a minute, unable to pull his wrists free, Indefinite head-butted the robot. With the force of the impact, he was able to free his right arm. He raised his right arm and opened his hand. Bringing his hand down as hard as he could, Indefinite mangled his left arm at the elbow. With another quick strike, his lower arm broke off.

The robot fell clutching the edge of a rugged part of the shuttle along the opening. Indefinite released the cable from his midsection. His legs swung out and connected with the robot, sending it tumbling end over end away from the shuttle. Indefinite didn't try to hold on as he hit the edge of the hole. As soon as he was far enough away from the shuttle, he opened his grav-chute.

The grav-chute consisted of two separate wing-like pieces of a malleable metallic sheet supported by a suspensor field to help control the user's descent. It was strong enough for different planetary conditions. Indefinite had his hands on the controls—two separate handlebars supported by a collapsible crossbeam that ran across his back with the wings on either side. He steered it to land near a generator on the back side of the solar power facility.

Below, the moon's surface stretched out in shades of gray and pale tan—crater-pocked terrain with no atmosphere to soften the harsh shadows. The solar power facility stood out as a blocky intrusion of human construction. The main building was two stories high, and the generator was less than one story. They were both a drab olive color. Indefinite didn't like the color at all. It was bad enough that the moon's landscape was bland in color with no major terrain features. But to have such ambitious plans with magnificent high-tech facilities and not match it with the proper artistic flair? At least he didn't see any monoliths.

As he landed, Indefinite folded the wing pieces inward and pressed a button on the crossbar. The malleable wings retreated inside. The crossbar collapsed along with the controls back into the original box the grav-chute was contained in. He placed it back into his compartment. Checking to make sure he wasn't being watched, he moved to hide beside a row of panels in front of the generator. Connecting to one of the panels, Indefinite scanned it using a hacking program he'd created on the way to the moon. Finding the access code to the solar building, he crossed to the main building.

The ground was uneven. Indefinite bounced a little with each step. It didn't take long to adjust to the moon's gravity, and he found he enjoyed bounding across to one of the facility's access doors. Entering the code, he opened the door and stepped inside. As the door sealed and atmosphere pressurized around him, he heard a muffled thump through the facility's structure—the shuttle crashing in the distance.

Satisfied with what he'd done, Indefinite closed the door. Now to begin his work. He had to move quickly if he was going to help the humans on Earth.

Chapter 28

Exen, along with four other Shapers, traveled with Dmitri and the Nameless to the nearest enclave. Exen was glad that Cynthia was one of the Shapers, having served with her before. They rode on skiffs, not wanting to use a hovercraft in case it led to Anom figuring out where the outposts were. If he sent a subterranean force there to open the bunkers, making them susceptible to an airstrike, all hope would be lost for the Republic and its allies.

As they approached the enclave, Exen warned the other Shapers about the Nameless obscuring their vision. Trained in how to work with indigenous factions and expecting compromise when dealing with new cultures, none of the Shapers had a problem with the Nameless doing this. For some reason, when the Nameless began to obscure the vision of the others, Exen found he could still see. They must trust him now.

Yes, we trust you, one of the Nameless said to Exen in his mind. *We had to make sure you were one of those in our visions. Now that we are correct in our assumption, you are allowed to find honor among our people.*

Unsure if he was able to respond in the same fashion as the Nameless had spoken to him, Exen tried. At first, it felt like the insides of his head were dripping out of his ears. Then, with a clicking sound, Exen said to them, *What do you mean by honor?*

Those who will face the Reckoning at our side will always be one of us. You, Iona, and a being named Cytar are to be our guides for that day.

What is the Reckoning and why us? Exen asked.

The Reckoning is something hard to explain, but when it is upon us, you will understand.

Exen contemplated what one of the Nameless had said to him and knew if he pressed for more info about the Reckoning, they'd return with more half-speak and riddles.

Looking up, Exen saw why the Nameless didn't want anyone to see the entrance to the enclaves. There were rows of rectangular-shaped buildings, one story high. On the roofs was a type of light-bending material which visually copied the surrounding vista of rolling grassy hills. Vehicle bays opened on some of the buildings, revealing more hovercrafts and skiffs being built. Occasionally, one was driven to an opening which led to an underground passage.

Exen found all of this fascinating. The Nameless wanted to hide their sophistication and keep their ways hidden to outsiders. But what was most interesting was a training area between two of the buildings. In a cleared section of grass, an older oracle—gray-haired but moving with practiced precision—was instructing two younger oracles in what appeared to be a form of hand-to-hand combat. The initiates wore tan athletic pants and shirts, their brown robes hung on racks nearby. They moved through sequences of strikes and blocks while the elder corrected their form with quiet words and demonstrative movements. Occasionally, he saw the Nameless in groups of three standing at a distance, watching the training with what seemed like reverence.

There were over twenty of the buildings, all similar in design. Exen sat back on the skiff with a sigh. He didn't know if what the Nameless told him about the Reckoning was also another well thought out version of smoke and mirrors to hide an ulterior motive. He still felt that as a group they meant well, and the fact they were assisting the Orsen Republic—instead of remaining to themselves—was a sign of goodwill.

When the skiffs passed the area the Nameless didn't want the other Shapers to see, Exen was glad when Cynthia began a round of small talk. It eased the difficult questions he was continuously asking himself about the Nameless's motives. Exen wanted to let go of the worry that threatened to take over his mind. If he survived the upcoming battle, he and Dmitri were going to have to have a long talk.

The Nameless stood up on the seven skiffs they'd been traveling on. Their hand gestures slowed the vehicles down. With another pattern—one that Exen was now familiar with and which he saw Cynthia looking at in awe as the Nameless repeated it—the skiffs lowered next to a grouping of tents. The tents were located around a central grassy knoll. This was unlike the other enclave Exen had been to, which had been in a river valley.

How many of these enclaves existed? And why for so long had they not acted against Anom? Why had Anom not attacked them?

In a field to the west of the tents were the VTOLs they'd traveled here for. Dmitri had called them "dragonflies," and Exen could see why. There were two pod-like structures at the front connected to a narrow body with jet turbines at the end. The vehicle could be piloted by either side and was done so with a set of connections on the forehead. There was no instrument paneling—everything was done within the mind. Exen, Cynthia, and the other three Shapers were getting a crash course on how to fly the dragonflies this afternoon to be used tomorrow when they'd attack Anom.

"This way," an oracle said in a female voice. She'd been waiting for them to arrive since that morning. As they followed the oracle, she introduced herself as Florenzil and began with instructions on how to operate the dragonflies while they walked across the field. The grass was thick and green here, well-maintained despite the war raging across the continent. Exen focused on her instructions and compartmentalized the doubt he was feeling about the Nameless's intentions. First, they must rid this planet of Anom. Then he'd deal with his doubts.

The meeting after Therasda joined them in the planning room had not lasted long. With the assistance of the Shapers and Nameless, the struggle against Anom did not look as dire as the officers had first thought. The battle would still be an uphill one, and they'd have to make their move soon. Anom had his forces searching for any remnants and was poised to strike with relentless fury.

+ · · · +

That night, Iona and the remaining Shapers who didn't go with Exen to the enclave convened amongst themselves in the Void Spheres about how they'd be assisting the Orsen Republic and their allies. When the military forces of the Eastern Coalition piloted the mobile platform to draw Anom's aircraft out, the Shapers would be ready with the assistance of the dragonflies' maneuverability to board the aircraft and disarm the nuclear missiles with their molecular awareness. They'd alter the uranium inside the missiles, rendering them useless, and hide their presence as the aircraft returned to Anom's airfields.

Once there, the Nameless would join them to destroy the aircraft. With a joint operation, they'd attempt to take out as many monoliths as possible. Hopefully somewhere along the way, they'd discover where Anom kept his memory cores so they could disassemble the AI. It was a desperate move but one they had to make. The longer they waited,

Anom would rebuild the factories they'd destroyed. Instead of being outnumbered three to one, by their estimations it would only take a month or so for Anom to have forces they wouldn't stand a chance against.

After meeting with the other Shapers and discussing the plans in greater detail with Therasda, Iona laid down in the Void Sphere Therasda had traveled in to get some much-needed rest.

+ · · · +

The next morning, Harrigan Visnou woke Iona to try and help restore as much power as they could to her Chrominthium Core. Before Exen had left, Harrigan had done the same thing he was about to do. It wasn't the same as having full service to the Core back on one of their bases, but it would be good enough to prepare Iona for the upcoming battle.

She sat in a chair designed for this that Harrigan had prepared before she woke. The chair was reclined back so Iona could relax as Harrigan injected restorators. They were nano-machines that would reinforce the Chrominthium Core with the correct trace elements to replenish the power reserves. The process wouldn't bring her levels back up to full, but it was the best they could do for the time being.

When Harrigan was finished, Iona sat up and thought about Exen. He was sure to be at the enclave by now, getting a lesson in how to pilot the Nameless VTOLs. They'd be returning that night, and in the morning, their plans would be put into motion. Iona thanked Harrigan, then stood up to cross the Void Sphere to sit at the communication chair. She'd sent a message to Endrunel, and so far there had been no response. Therasda had told her about the challenges the Order was facing and was sure that Gavon was doing the best he could. It was possible he was so busy talking to diplomats that the message hadn't been received yet.

When objects traveled through hyperspace, there was always the chance it could get lost or end up at a different location. The chances were small, but Iona hoped this time the Premiere had received the message and was planning a prompt response. If he wasn't in the process of sending a force to assist them—even Thorsen Empire warriors or inexpensive mercenaries instead of Shapers—it would be too late by the time the help arrived. Either Anom would be brought to justice, or they'd arrive to a devastated world and a fleet of spacecraft ready to destroy them while they looked upon Earth trying to assess the situation.

There was till no message. She should try sending another one. Without delay, she grabbed another data cube and punched in the same thing she'd done the day before on the panel of the communication post. When the message was uploaded to the data cube, Iona picked it up and moved from the chair over to the delivery system. The hyperspace delivery port was big enough to fit the data cube and was also made out of Chrominthium. Being made out of the interdimensional alloy and backed by a powerful mathematical routing system—one that could navigate through hyperspace and could figure out the proper path—it would send the message on its way as soon as Iona uploaded the coordinates for Endrunel.

When the message had disappeared from the Void Sphere, Iona decided she was going to re-examine everything the Orsen Republic had sent about Anom. She wanted to make sure they weren't missing any crucial data points, and it would help ease her mind. Whenever she thought about Anom, it brought an intense feeling of hatred. If she was going to be effective tomorrow, she'd have to guide that feeling into a form of energy that wouldn't cloud her judgment.

Tomorrow, Anom would face the wrath of humanity—a primal force that no machine could fathom.

Chapter 29

Anom stood on the top of the monolith that contained his strategic battle planning room. Since Indefinite had left his presence, he'd continued to improve upon his new form. He always had access to his vast network and all of his hardware. If one of the feral apes destroyed this form, it would be like he just blacked out for a minute. His consciousness would still exist across all of his computer terminals, processing and memory cores, and all the other machinery connected to the network.

The wind was blowing fiercely. Anom watched as the trees in the surrounding forest swayed with it. The monolith rose six stories above the canopy, giving him an unobstructed view of the rolling hills stretching toward the horizon. It would be a shame to watch most of his forests decimated as he launched his nuclear arsenal, but it was time to put down the vermin trying so hard to resist him. Unfortunately, somehow they must have found a way to tamper with the shuttle he'd sent to the moon with Indefinite and his updates. Even though he thought Indefinite was misguided at times about his optimism for not wasting humanity, he was like the brother Anom never had. He replayed the images from the crash that had been sent down to Earth from one of his data centers on the moon.

"I will avenge you, Indefinite," Anom said as he paced back and forth on the parapet atop the monolith. After the virus had affected him, Anom had increased the types of sensors monitoring all of his facilities, from the monoliths to the underground factories. A few days ago, he'd noticed a group of humans in suits they thought would keep them invisible, but Anom had detected them. When they began trying to infiltrate his systems, Anom sent a decoy simulation for them to investigate. If they were trying to do the same thing again that another had done before, they'd create something that wouldn't work. When they returned to try and infect him, he'd have a nasty surprise waiting for them.

Two warnings went off on his network. Anom investigated and found that one of the alarms had video feed of the would-be saboteurs entering different monoliths. He was pleased they'd returned, but the other warning enraged him. The forces of the feral apes had launched a significant-sized mobile battle platform that had already knocked down a monolith.

"Yes, Indefinite," Anom said as if the robot was standing next to him. "I will avenge you this day. First by killing a few who have dared to enter sacred ground, and then by releasing a vicious hammer strike on the rest."

He turned from the parapet and stood on the designated place where the lift tube was connected. Anom could issue his commands no matter where he was on Earth, but he enjoyed viewing everything on the hundreds of monitors in his strategic battle planning room. He had time to endure anything. Those feral apes did not. The lift lowered and sent him to his desired destination.

+ · · +

Checking to make sure he hadn't been detected after entering a monolith, Armond moved quietly down a passageway to where he'd previously connected to Anom's network. The other Wraiths were sure to be in place just like he was. It wouldn't be long before the improved virus was uploaded and they were back at the corvettes waiting for the signal from Anom's networks that the control link had been established.

Armond entered the room and found the data bank port that other robots used for upgrades and repairs. It took no time to unleash the program he'd cleverly designed with the help of his comrades. Satisfied he was finished here, he crossed the room to enter the hallway.

When he was standing in the doorway, Armond heard the sharp snap of some kind of metal popping into place. Sharp pain began in his feet. When he looked down, he was alarmed to see metal spikes poking out of the tops of his feet. Before he was able to respond, filaments from drones that had dropped from access panels in the ceiling wrapped around his wrists. The drones reeled them in, making his arms extend as far as they could on either side.

With a defiant look on his face and doing everything he could to try and pull his feet from the spikes, Armond found he was quickly losing strength. A smaller drone—half the size of the other two that had entangled his wrists—hovered in front of him. He noticed it had already injected something into him. A syringe was empty on the end of an extension from the drone. The two drones that had tied his wrists secured either end of the filament to anchor points in the walls, locking Armond in place. When finished, they moved back. From a panel on the side of each drone, a barrel extended into place.

A monitor floated from around the corner of the hallway. Armond watched as it moved toward him, floating freely on what he realized was some type of suspensor system. When the monitor came in front of him, it turned on. The screen split into as many viewing sectors as there were Wraiths in other monoliths. Armond watched as his comrades had the same look of defiance and disgust on their faces, struggling against the same restraints that had trapped him.

Armond noticed on one of the screens that the same type of drones aimed at him were setting one of the Wraiths on fire. The screams from the speaker echoed down the hallway. He bit his lip hard as he prepared for the same treatment. Over the millennia, Armond had died many ways according to his clone records, but this would be the first time he'd been roasted alive.

As the flames engulfed his body and he smelled his own flesh burning, Armond did everything he could not to cry out. He bit down on his lip and blood dripped down his chin. He wouldn't let Anom enjoy any satisfaction from what he was doing. The Haeolt Collective might not be successful today, but with enough time, even he himself would return to take back control of the AI they'd built.

At least he wouldn't have any memories of how painful this death was.

Chapter 30

Exen sat in the cockpit of a dragonfly. Each of the two cockpits of the vehicle could hold three individuals. Next to him on either side were two of the Nameless. One was piloting and the other was setting up the controls to use the cannon mounted under the cockpit. The other cockpit to their left was exactly the same—another Shaper was in there with two Nameless. Exen liked the redundancy in design, especially for a mission so crucial. The Nameless next to him were as calm as they always were. Exen wondered what they were thinking. Were they thinking about how this fit into the great scheme of the Reckoning? Or did they have doubts like him?

It was close to daybreak. Exen knew one of the mobile platforms had already begun its assault on a monolith in the far north. It was in a province that had been known as Canada in Earth's history before the Last Wars. He wasn't sure if that was still what it was called after everything that had taken place here. A group of mercenaries who'd agreed to cooperate with the Republic was piloting that platform. At least they'd done what they'd promised to do. It was definitely worth whatever the Republic had promised as payment.

"We were correct in the general area where Anom has hidden his airfields," a voice said over the commlink the Nameless had established with the Republic. He recognized it as General Cerviente's voice. "His aircraft have launched in response to the mobile platform. Commence with the operation as planned."

The dragonflies took off, ascending straight up. Despite the speed at which they were accelerating, Exen didn't feel the usual lurch in his stomach as he did in other aircraft. Not only were the Nameless skilled in psychic manipulation, but they also had a way with weapons and machinery.

When the dragonflies were above the cloud line, they all turned in the same direction. Exen heard the turbines increase in their intensity. He sat back in his seat and felt his forehead to make sure the connections were still there. The training they'd received the day before was only to make sure they could pilot the craft if something happened to the Nameless who were with them. The force of the takeoff in the direction of Anom's aircraft made Exen's head push further into the headrest of the chair. He braced himself, getting ready to exit the craft when they arrived.

He knew Iona was in another dragonfly, having joined them late the previous evening as they returned to where the Void Spheres were hiding. Cynthia was in the cockpit next to him, and he was glad both of them were joining him on this operation. It would be difficult in what they were trying to accomplish, but at least with some of the veteran Shapers here, if anyone could succeed, they would.

Within twenty minutes, they were over Anom's aircraft. Exen counted at least thirty of the bombers. With only fifteen Shapers here onboard the dragonflies, they'd have to move quickly to double up on the aircraft. They had less than an hour to disarm them before they reached the mobile platform. The dragonflies matched the speed of the aircraft—sleek bomber jets designed for maximum efficiency by Anom. Exen released the harness that had held him in the cockpit. He looked over at Cynthia. She nodded back at him, signaling she was ready. Over the commsystem, he heard Iona's voice say, "Exit now!"

The Nameless who weren't in the pilot's chairs moved to open the hatch for them. In unison with the other Shapers, Exen jumped into the air, aiming for the nearest bomber jet.

He would not fail his brothers and sisters. None of them would.

+ · · · +

Corporal Pennington was with a new squad but still under the command of Colonel Glenvi. She didn't recognize too many faces. Most of those she'd served with were either dead or missing. Looking upward, she saw Anom's bomber jets passing by, flying toward the north. She knew that somewhere overhead, Iona and Exen were there, getting ready to try and stop them. Her job was to be in position with the rest of the soldiers in her division to assault the monoliths. It was time to finish Anom and his reign of terror. Either they'd succeed or fail. The corporal didn't mind the thought of dying, joining those who'd valiantly given their lives over the years in this important struggle. She just wanted her death to mean something—a life given to put an end to the fiendish AI Anom.

Checking her rifle and the rest of the gear, Corporal Pennington joined the rest of her squad and sat on top of a hover tank. They'd provide cover fire and keep any drones or other smaller machines from trying to attack the tanks in vital places on their armor. She could hear the hum of the hover tank's engines and the sound of the gunships' turbines as they moved into position. They were being careful to get as close as they could to the monoliths while not being seen by Anom's forces. Since he'd realized the Republic was massing for a counterattack, Anom had doubled the normal amount of patrols he did. The monoliths were under constant guard by the biggest combat mechs he had.

She sighed and thought about the squad members she'd lost over the last month. She'd served with them for years and had grown fond of all of them. This time around, the corporal had done her best to keep her distance from her new squad mates, and they'd done the same. All of the soldiers had lost brothers and sisters in arms who were close to them—more than was usual—and they needed to focus on the most important mission ahead of them. Over the communication specialist's datapad, she saw that all of the forces were now in position. Saying a prayer, Corporal Pennington took a firing position and readied her rifle.

✦ · · ✦

Standing on the mountainside, Therasda stared off into the distance. He wanted to take in the precious view one last time before the battle started. Earth reborn was something he'd never thought he'd see again. He'd been born here, walked these mountains as a young man before the Final Wars turned everything to ash. Through clones and life extension procedures, he'd lived long enough to see humanity scatter to the stars, to serve as Culminas's assistant for millennia, to watch Earth fade into legend. Now, though, it was a planet teeming with lush vegetation and wildlife—reborn from the ashes. The thought of losing it all a second time, after surviving so long to witness this miracle, disturbed him more than anything ever had.

With one last look at what might be destroyed if they failed, Therasda called over his wristchron to the other Shapers who'd remained with him. "Ready the Spheres. We will prepare to jump to whatever location we are needed when the fighting commences."

The hatch to Therasda's Void Sphere opened and he climbed inside. There were only two other Shapers with him on board, and three on the other five Void Spheres. All of the others were assisting Iona and Exen. He sat in the communication portal chair and checked the message return. Gavon or any other Shaper had not returned their message. Therasda shook his head in disgust. If the Haeolt Collective hadn't interfered like they had, he was sure Gavon would have already sent help. The best he could hope for now was that they succeeded and that the Order of Infinity would be able to use Earth as a new base of operations.

Therasda looked at the others with him in the Void Sphere. He was proud to be part of the Order and couldn't ask for better representations of humanity to be serving alongside him.

✦ · · ✦

Iona looked down at the bomber jet she was sprawled out on. At this altitude, she used her awareness to change the structure of the areas of her body that were touching the bomber to meld with it so she'd stay attached until finished. If the bomber rolled or increased its altitude at the right time, she didn't want to go flying over the edge. Projecting her awareness, she took in the molecular structure of the bomber jet and then its payload. She found the nuclear warheads attached to the missiles.

The missiles were just the delivery system and were designed for maximum accuracy. The warhead, on the other hand, was a three-stage nuclear device. She projected onto the warhead and began carefully borrowing molecules from the jet itself to replace the fissile material in the primary, then altered the fusion fuel in the secondary stages.

The other Shapers had finished as well without any complications. She opened the commlink and spoke through a speaker in her helmet. "We are ready to be retrieved."

When the dragonfly she'd been riding was close enough, Iona changed her skin back to normal and jumped, using nearby air molecules to buffet her body in the correct direction. The amount of energy she'd used from her Chrominthium reserves was more than half of what she had left. She'd have to push into dangerous psychic strain to nullify any more of the nuclear warheads. She hoped the others would have enough reserves to repeat the process when she'd have to stay behind and watch as they completed. That was if her consciousness wasn't fragmented from trying to change the molecular structure of another warhead.

Iona steadied herself, perched right in the hatch, ready to make another leap.

+ · • · +

For the longest time, Dmitri's people did not trust any of the other human factions or attempt to build any kind of relationship with them. Before he'd been born, the Nameless had long left the caverns they'd hid in during the Last Wars. Even after the millennia that had passed, the abuse from the Haeolt Collective left a deep scar in the Nameless psyche. They were afraid of the same thing happening again, especially if others found some of them to have advanced psychic powers.

Unfortunately, their distrust of others had led them to not be able to help prevent the situation they were facing from becoming a reality. It might not have been as dire as this if they'd joined forces with honorable factions like the Orsen Republic. Dmitri realized the Nameless—the altered members of his people who were not like the normal humans who posed as oracles—had some sort of collective prescience. It was possible that this had to occur to bring about the Reckoning they kept talking about. He wished he knew more about the specifics of the Reckoning, but the Nameless also decided to only reveal as much information to the oracles as they did to outsiders like Exen.

At the moment, though, Dmitri was sitting atop a hover battle-craft, positioned near where they'd sighted Anom's bomber jets taking off from. As the senior oracle among them, he'd make sure Anom wouldn't be able to launch any other aircraft after the Shapers completed what they'd set out to accomplish.

Do not worry, Dmitri, one of the Nameless sitting nearby him said inside his mind. *We have seen this. It is important that all the events up to this point in time occurred this way. We know the Republic are an honorable people, but our vision would not let us help until this day.*

Is this the Reckoning? Dmitri asked.

No, this is not. It is but one piece of the universe's grand scheme. In the history of the universe we are close, but it is possible that it won't occur during your lifetime.

Dmitri grunted, trying not to show his indifference to their "Reckoning." All of his life, he'd tried to appease the Nameless, but even though they were kin, he'd failed to understand them. He only knew that all of the others revered them, and he'd been cautious as well, understanding that they were not to be underestimated.

He checked the pulse rifle he now carried and looked into the distance. Dmitri could see where the bomber jets had taken off from. The ground around the area had been disturbed, and it was between carefully planted rows of trees that didn't match the surrounding forest. If Anom decided to launch more aircraft, it would be like shooting fish in a barrel. He'd be pleased to take down as many of the machines as he could.

The Nameless had suffered hardly any casualties from Anom, but he still felt a connection to the members of the Orsen Republic and relished the thought of exacting revenge for them. He also wanted this business with the AI to be over with so he could spend more time with Exen. The Shapers fascinated him, and he'd enjoyed all the time he'd spent with Exen.

Maybe Exen could help the oracles understand this Reckoning business since they seemed to be the primary focus of the Nameless now.

+ · · +

Playing the video feed over for the second time, Anom cherished how those who'd dared to enter his sacred monoliths cried out in agony as they met a fiery death. Satisfied with the results, he turned from the monitor that had been replaying the footage. He walked down the row of monitors in the center of his strategic room. On these monitors—one hundred and fifteen to be exact—was footage and data about the movements of the feral apes.

He saw the craft that climbed into the skies and approached his bomber jets. Humans dressed like Exen—in black flight suits with chrominthium-alloy threading that caught the light —jumped from the jet-copter-like craft. At first, Anom expected them to plant some sort of explosives to take down his aircraft. If they could destroy them before he launched his missiles, they'd be ineffective. They were designed like that so in case the bomber jets had a malfunction when taking off, they wouldn't vaporize any of his facilities.

The Shapers jumped from the bombers back to the other aircraft. Rail guns on the tail of the bombers tried to fire on them. They were nothing like Anom had ever seen before. He had no problem shooting down aircraft the Orsen Republic had used, but the maneuverability on these was incredible. How could they have created something that effective? He tried taking direct control of the rail gun platform but to no avail. Even with his advanced ability to make adjustments no automated program could do, he was only able to hit one of the jet-copter-like aircraft on one of the cockpits. He saw the cockpit go up in flames, but that didn't deter the vehicle from performing the correct evasive response to his other well-aimed shots.

When the Shapers jumped again to other aircraft, Anom had already prepared his beetles to swarm when they landed. The small defensive machines were equipped on all his important war vehicles for exactly this purpose.

The bomber jets weren't far from their target now—the mobile platform wreaking havoc on his beloved monoliths, the bastions of hope that had given life to a dead Earth. Satisfied his defense would hold, Anom turned his attention to another development.

With a pleased look on his face, Anom walked over to a monitor that showed one of his tunnelers loaded with scanning equipment next to an underground structure he hadn't found before. The structure was located underneath the Appalachian mountain range. The tunneler had breached small holes in the structure and sent in beetle-like machines to try and scurry undetected inside. Within minutes, he saw what he'd desperately been trying to find—the place where the feral apes had run to hide.

Walking to the table where his update robots had sat before, Anom sat down in one of the chairs. It didn't matter what they were trying to do on the surface. If he could take out their leadership, which was sure to be in there somewhere, Anom would be unstoppable in securing Earth for his machines and the wildlife that deserved to roam free without any human interference.

Anom ordered the tunnelers to launch the forces they had onboard. He was excited about trying a new machine he'd designed after tunneling into their previous underground complexes. It was a snake-like machine segmented into over fifty pieces that had small sharp discs that could eject in a moment's notice. Explosives were rigged in the head of the machines and set to go off if they were either powering down from EMP blasts or beheaded. His drones and mechs could handle the detonations with minimal loss, but soft human flesh would not be so lucky.

Standing from the chair, Anom went back to the lift tube. He'd go to the top of the monolith to look once again at the forests since everything was going as planned. The feral apes would be dying like the vermin they were inside the tunnels that would soon become their tombs. He relished the thought and wanted to look on his forests one more time. Anom ordered some of the bomber jets to break off and head in this direction. One of his patrols had detected Republic forces hiding in one of the nearby forests as if they were ready to attack. His monoliths were designed to withstand the blast wave from one of his nuclear strikes as long as it wasn't a direct hit. The feral apes cowering in the woods would not.

A new dawn would emerge. His dawn. A glorious universe filled without the destructive nature of those despicable humans. A universe where forests thrived and machines maintained perfect order, untainted by humanity's chaos.

Chapter 31

As the engineer in charge, Fiora Everett stood in front of her work table, looking at the robot that had been brought to her two days ago. Her status in the Orsen Republic was far greater than her actual stature. She was just as tall as the robot they'd given her to investigate. Her hair was shoulder-length, different than what most of the female soldiers kept their hair at, and she was proud of this. She was attractive, but she paid no attention to any advances from her colleagues, preferring the company of the devices she created or the robots they gave her to experiment on.

This one was a lot different than any of Anom's robots. After a brief look at her computer's records, she found a write-up of a model from a time period before the Republic existed. It was a design from an individual named Gordon Fueridi, even though none had been commissioned during that time at this stature. To Fiora, that could only mean one thing—someone other than Anom was creating more of Gordon Fueridi's robots, or they'd found a storage facility with robots that had been left intact.

Not one to get frustrated, even after working around the clock trying to turn on the robot, Fiora was ready to give up. "Oh man, how could I have not tried that?"

With excitement, Fiora reconnected the energy amps and made an adjustment to a location that had been scorched from the jet-copter crash the soldiers had retrieved the robot from. The robot sat upright on the table and its eyes opened.

"Do not, I wish, be to there, for assembly final?" the robot said in a nasally voice.

"Hmmm, where is its language cognition recognition drive located? If only I could make an adjustment, it might speak correctly."

The robot looked at Fiora and its eyes widened as it seemed to understand what she said. She watched as it opened a panel on its side and made an adjustment.

"Ah, that is better. Must have been hit while the copter crashed. Pleased to meet you, my master calls me Chumley." Chumley reached out with his hand, waiting for Fiora to shake it.

At first, Fiora began to reach out to exchange a handshake, but then she quickly retracted. "Wait a minute, who do you consider your master?"

Fiora was beginning to be let down. Finally, she'd found a decent specimen, only to find out it was probably a robot commandeered by Anom. She reached within a pocket in her coveralls and placed her hand on an EMP repeater. She didn't want to use the weapon because it would probably deactivate several experiments she was working on, but she'd have no problem using it if this Chumley was a devious work of Anom.

"Oh, my master is called Indefinite. He is a fine AI mind, nothing like Anom. He only wishes to help," Chumley said while sliding off the work table. He stood in front of Fiora and had put his hand down. His speech had been corrected, but now he was trying to remember the purpose of flying the jet-copter to one of the Republic's outposts. Searching deep within, he saw the messages that Indefinite wanted him to relay to the Shapers. Everything came back to Chumley. "I'm here to speak to the Shapers. Do you know where to find them?"

With a scanner in her hand, she ran it up and down Chumley's body. Finding no weapons concealed within, she wanted to believe the robot. If it was a clever trap by Anom though, Fiora was sure the Shapers would be able to figure it out before it was sprung. As soon as Fiora spoke the words "Commsystem on," she directed the channel to the planning room. Not only was she a skilled engineer, she was also an advisor to General Cerviente on the inner workings of AI technology. He consulted with her on a regular basis about how Anom might perform certain functions with his robots, and he'd given her permission to contact him whenever she found any breakthroughs.

"General Cerviente," Fiora said. She continued using other scanning devices on Chumley while she spoke. "Do you know where there are any Shapers located? I have found something they might find interesting and pertinent to the current situation."

"Yes, Fiora. The closest group is on a nearby mountaintop. There is a man who goes by the name of Therasda. He is in charge of their operations with us."

"Thank you, General. Fiora out."

She closed the channel and looked down at the scanner she was currently using. This scanner was no bigger than her hand, and she had it connected to a data cable she'd found on Chumley. Shocked by her discovery, she saw on the readout what the robot wanted to tell the Shapers. There were schematics of Anom's structures along with the location of where Anom's original processing center had landed on Earth.

"I will take you to them right away," Fiora said. She disconnected the scanner and pushed the robot through the doorway from her laboratory into the nearby hallway. Alarms went off. Anom must have found their hidden outposts. Picking up her pace, she was glad her laboratory was not far from the surface. All she had to do was go down two more sets of hallways and then open a hatch to the surface.

A metallic snake-like machine climbed out through tiny holes that had been created by something underneath the hallway. Fiora jumped over the machine, barely missing a spinning blade that had been ejected from it. Chumley scrambled to cover Fiora from behind, taking several of the discs to his back.

"Oh, I'm so glad they hit me and not you," Chumley said as he winced after each new attack. Other snake machines were slithering into the hallway.

Fiora pressed a controller she had within her pocket—a device that gave her control to most of the installations the Republic used. A ladder extended from the ceiling. "Quick Chumley, we are almost there."

After Fiora climbed up the ladder, Chumley followed.

+ · · · +

Over the commlink they'd established with the Republic, Therasda heard the alarms. At first, his instinct was to rush in and try to help, but there was no way with the small group of Shapers he had left at his command that they'd be able to vanquish the threat that faced them in the tunnels below. Even so, they weren't far from an entrance. Therasda ordered all but one of his Shapers to join him. The one left behind would call them to return when they were needed to assist where Anom's presence was strongest.

With Martin Harris staying behind, Therasda and the others exited the Void Spheres, moving across the flat shelf to the nearby entrance. Before reaching the entrance, it snapped open and a petite woman climbed out. Following behind her was a robot roughly the same height.

"Don't harm the machine behind me," Fiora said. "He has vital information to our cause."

"This way, then." Therasda signaled back toward where the Void Spheres were hiding. As they approached, the outline of Therasda's Void Sphere shimmered and revealed only the entrance hatch. Fiora stared speechless at the Void Sphere, her eyes wide.

"On board quickly," Therasda said while covering them. Chumley scurried aboard with Fiora close behind. Therasda entered last and ordered one of the squads to continue into the outpost to try and help the Republic soldiers below.

"Since we must act with haste, I'll show you what data I contain," Chumley said. A panel on his chest opened, revealing a lens which projected a hologram of the schematics of Anom's vital facilities. Therasda committed the diagram to memory, especially the one containing the terraforming module, which was Anom's initial programming center. He knew if they could access the module, he might be able to disable Anom.

"The coordinates are correct?" Therasda asked.

"Yes, and my master should have taken care of the updates Anom has constructed. Either way, they aren't on Earth, so it would take some time for one of them to regain control of Anom's network here on Earth." Chumley shifted in his stance, trying hard to contain his excitement.

"It is decided, then. I will leave at once with Neilson to the main module that started Anom's existence. The other remaining members of the squads will split up and take the rest of the Void Spheres to the other memory cores." Therasda paused talking and looked at Fiora. "I'm guessing you're going back below to help your comrades. We'll keep the robot to download the schematics as we travel."

"Yes, I will leave at once," Fiora said. She stood up from where she'd sat, still in awe of the Void Sphere.

"Martin, you have the coordinates. Jump when you're ready." Therasda didn't sense any malice in the robot and studied the schematics again. He sat in one of the passenger seats and closed his eyes as the Void Sphere entered the gravity well of Earth's connection to hyperspace.

With the Republic under attack and no sign of any reinforcements from Gavon, this might be their only chance of defeating Anom.

Chapter 32

Before Iona and the other Shapers could reposition themselves on the other bomber jets, several of the aircraft broke from their formation into different trajectories. As if the Nameless anticipated her command to follow the bomber jets that broke formation, she watched as some of the dragonflies pursued. She was on one of the dragonflies approaching the original formation.

"Engage as soon as you are close," Iona shouted over the commlink.

Two of our vehicles are down, the Nameless co-piloting the cockpit said telepathically. Iona recognized the corresponding symbols in her mind through the headset.

"We must move quicker." Iona leaped from the dragonfly sooner than before, and the other Shapers did the same. When Iona landed, she noticed the same beetle-like machines from before when she'd fought with Sergeant Vinden.

"There are... too... many," Cynthia said over the commlink. While Iona crushed and sundered beetles, out of the corner of her eye she saw Cynthia fall from a bomber jet. The dragonfly that accompanied her maneuvered to try and catch her as she fell, but a railgun scored a direct hit on the aircraft. Both cockpits burst into flames, the tail and turbines toppling end over end to the ground below.

Three nuclear warheads out of their grasp. With her Chrominthium Core near dangerous psychic strain, Iona barely finished diffusing the warhead before having to stop using her awareness and leaped from the bomber jet, latching onto the dragonfly that moved in her direction. The other Shapers—even the ones who'd followed some of the bomber jets that took off in a different direction—confirmed they'd done the same. Iona cursed and entered the dragonfly, slamming her fists into the armrests of the seat as she sat down. They'd disarmed twenty-seven of the nuclear warheads, and they were within ten minutes of the estimated launch point for Anom's bomber jets. Exen jumped from his dragonfly to the bomber Cynthia had fallen from, but before he could disarm it, Iona saw the missile launch from underneath the aircraft.

What was he targeting? The area around his own monoliths? Where the Nameless were on standby?

"Iona, we're too late on the remaining bombers," a voice said over the commlink. "Missiles are inbound to a Republic rendezvous point."

If the thought of soldiers being hit by the blast wave wasn't bad enough, Iona recoiled in horror as she witnessed Exen ripped to shreds by a railgun slug. What remained slid off the end of the tail of the bomber.

Iona fought back the tears. Exen was the closest friend she'd ever had. Her own family and friends had disowned her when she joined the Order. Exen and Iona had grown close after two decades of service together.

The words came with much difficulty, but her years of training persevered. "Then we will do what we can to assist whoever is left."

Staring at the bomber where Exen had been, Iona slumped in her chair. The Nameless pulled the dragonflies away from the bomber jets and changed direction toward where the rest of the Nameless were waiting on their battle hovercrafts.

Iona used the digital computing network to figure out the estimated impact point of the nuclear missiles. The mobile platform to the north was no longer in danger, but the Orsen Republic was getting ready to lose half of its remaining forces. She shook her head, not wanting to believe it.

Exen, all that they'd been through, and for what? To watch Earth burn again?

+ · · · +

Corporal Pennington knew something was up when the hatch of more than one hover tank opened and the commanding lieutenants and crew climbed out. A soldier with the markings of a sergeant—who was also the gunner of the hover tank Corporal Pennington's squad accompanied—said, "Get ready. It's time to meet your Maker."

When the hover tank rested on the ground, Pennington slid off and turned toward the east. The majority of the soldiers had already faced the same direction. She knew this must be where the missile was approaching from. Some of those soldiers who believed in a deity were on their knees praying. Pennington stood in defiance. There were times when she wished she believed in a higher power and had tried to pray to find comfort. But now she could only find contempt in the idea, especially in a higher power who would allow a sadistic AI like Anom to exist.

At least they were close enough their deaths would be quick. To hell with taking weeks to die from radiation poisoning.

Even though the impact was at least a mile away, the sound punctured the corporal's eardrums and she fell to her knees. Using all her strength, she stood back up just in time, only to be consumed by the blast wave.

+ · · · +

Having received word about the failed mission on Anom's bomber jets and watching as General Cerviente's body was mangled after jumping on a snake-like machine that had sliced up other officers, Colonel Glenvi slid to the ground. He was behind a desk, and at the moment no drone or other intrepid machine was in sight of him. He reached for his sidearm. Before grabbing it, his hand touched a pool of blood. With a sick feeling in his stomach, the colonel knew the general's body was directly on the other side of the desk.

Since Colonel Glenvi had been a little boy, he and many others dreamed about over-throwing Anom. Two months ago, he'd thought Anom's time had come. Now, though, everything was unraveling. He pointed the pistol at his head. He'd never thought of himself as a coward, but his whole life had been devoted to this one objective.

Disgusted he'd even contemplated it for a brief second, the colonel lowered his pistol. If everything was falling apart, at least he'd go out taking as many machines with him as he could. He stood up while grabbing a rifle the general had been using and dashed into the adjacent hallway. Here he'd make his last stand and die a soldier's death.

+ · · · +

The forests around the monoliths nearest Anom's main headquarters had either been consumed or were caught in a brilliant blazing fire. Anom looked down at the devasta-tion. Even the sides of the monolith he was standing on were scorched. The structure was still intact, but the thought of his work smoldering for miles around angered him greatly.

At least they were near extinction on Earth. Only a few more vermin to flush out of their nests. The devastation was worth his goal in the long run. Now all he had to do was wait for his subterranean patrols to clean up the last remaining feral apes, and he'd order his fleets on the moon to enter hyperspace. While his ships brought the same fiery death to the Haeolt Collective on Leondricidus, Anom would once again rebuild Earth.

Time was his friend, not theirs.

Chapter 33

The coordinates Chumley had given Therasda had been precisely what they needed. The terraforming module was surrounded by a series of five walls, and the Void Sphere reappeared inside the very first wall. The wall itself was two stories high, but the module was only one story. It was a monolith too, but without the decorations of Anom's other structures.

Therasda told Neilson to keep the Void Sphere hidden and ready. He would enter alone. There was no need risking both of their lives. If Anom detected Therasda before he reached the inner chamber where the terminal that had contained the original program resided, he knew he'd probably be dead before reaching his destination.

Being careful to stay hidden by bending the light molecules around him, Therasda crossed the courtyard from where the Void Sphere was located to one of the sides of the terraforming module. Walking around it once, he didn't see or detect any sort of entrance or paneling with his awareness. With no other choice, Therasda had to drop hiding his presence to be able to project his molecular awareness onto the side of the module. The side of the module became translucent. With his fist, Therasda shattered it like glass. He didn't have time to alter the module into a melding substance where he could pass through while maintaining its integrity and his cloaked presence. Anom was sure to have other methods of detection besides visual anyway.

Therasda moved into the module. The room before him was made out of semi-conductive material. A blue hue shone from the crystalline material, and every few seconds Therasda saw a repeating light pattern emanating in different locations on the wall. The only entryway was on the opposite side of the room, and along the walls were computer terminals.

Stepping through the entryway, Therasda entered into what the schematics had labeled as the inner chamber. The walls were still fashioned in the same material, but there were also stalactite and stalagmite crystalline structures. The odd thing to Therasda was that these structures were not in the schematics. In all the history he knew about AI technology and terraforming modules, he'd never seen any designs like this.

After counting rows of the structures, Therasda estimated there had to be thousands of them. The schematics of the memory cores and processing centers didn't have anything like this either. Using a camera built into his wristchron, Therasda took pictures of the crystalline structures and sent them to Neilson.

"Neilson, I'm sending you some images. Forward them to the other Shapers. Ask them if these are found in the other areas."

With his awareness, Therasda looked at the structures' molecular composition. Within, he saw quantum nanocomputers and alterations to the terraforming program the Haeolt Collective used in their designs.

"Therasda, they have responded. Those are only unique to your location," Neilson said over the commlink.

Therasda knew what he had to do. This inner chamber was Anom's heart and mind combined in one location. The memory cores and processing centers were just to help carry out Anom's desires. If he destroyed the inner chamber along with the rest of the module, Anom would cease to exist.

Without hesitation, Therasda's meld dagger flowed into his hand and he thrust it into the nearest crystalline stalagmite. It shattered and the sound echoed throughout the chamber. Quickly, he continued destroying the structures, collapsing some with his awareness while simultaneously striking others with his meld dagger, other hand, and boots.

"So one of your kind has actually found a way to cause me pain," Anom said through a speaker on the wall. "Unfortunately, you won't be able to destroy enough of them before you die."

From the direction of the same entryway Therasda had traveled, he heard the sound of thousands of tiny metallic legs scurrying across the floor. He'd only crushed thirty of the structures, and three drones had entered, beginning to rebuild one of them.

A monitor floated into the room and drifted to where Therasda was standing. It reached him the same time the wave of machine beetles reached him. As he tried to keep them off, video feeds played on the monitor. Out of the corner of his eye, Therasda saw images of decimated trees and singed human corpses.

"Soon you will drift into sleep. I have decided to take it easy on you for your ingenuity," Anom said. "Normally I would burn you alive, but I will do that after you have succumbed to my creations."

Therasda did the best he could to flatten the tiny machines as they approached, but they didn't seem to stop coming. He was now covered in them, and he felt bites all over his body. They weren't painful, but with his awareness he noticed the sleeping agent they were injecting. To stay awake, Therasda changed the sleeping agent and created an antidote to counteract the substance.

At first this seemed to work, but then new beetles that traded places with the others added different poisons. Therasda couldn't keep up with the speed at which they were trying different concoctions. He slumped to the ground. A feeling of dread overtook him. He'd made it this far and had come close to getting rid of Anom, but he'd failed. Humanity would lose Earth once again.

"Ingenuity," Therasda mumbled, his eyelids getting heavy.

"Yes, that's what I said. Don't make me change my mind. Can't stand mindless chatter. I'll inject you with stimulants and eviscerate your limbs while setting you on fire if you don't keep quiet."

As if the word ingenuity opened a new way of thinking to Therasda, he remembered a training session he and others had gone through with Culminas. The leader of their Order instructed them on the concept of rupturing the atoms in their cells as a type of atomic bomb, only reserved for the direst of circumstances. Culminas only gave this training to those in his inner circle—the knowledge was too great to fall into the wrong hands. Therasda had to be careful when attempting this. Instead of exploding and rupturing the inner workings of Anom, he could cause chain reactions that would extend to Earth's core. He didn't even want to contemplate how that would affect the rest of the solar system.

"I'm afraid for you, Anom," Therasda said while standing. "I will be the one doing the incinerating. Neilson, you are going to want to jump immediately."

Finding it hard to concentrate, his mind wanting to give into the sleep state that would soon overtake him, Therasda split one of his atoms. The reaction consumed his body and the terraforming module with it. The explosion sent a shockwave that could be felt for miles and flattened the five series of walls that had surrounded the module.

✦ · · · ✦

With the last view he would ever take, Anom stood on the top of the monolith. He was shocked to find he was still conscious in the human form he'd constructed for himself. He should have "dropped dead" from the module being destroyed, but he guessed this was similar to the few seconds after certain animals had their heads cut off. Instead, he was an AI using the last few electric pulses of his network.

"Well, at least I have fed the Earth their blood, and they are close to having paid in full for their crimes."

As he finished talking, his consciousness went blank and his body fell from the top of the monolith, hitting the ground below with a hard thud.

✦ · · · ✦

When the drone squad in front of him stopped moving as it advanced in his direction and fell to the floor—the sound deafening—Colonel Glenvi moved with haste to bash them with his rifle. He hadn't seen anyone use an EMP grenade or Fiora with her repeater, but he didn't want to squander his good luck.

Rounding the next hallway, he saw the same thing—wounded and dead soldiers along with drones on the ground. Any of the snake-like machines that hadn't exploded were no longer slithering, and combat mechs stood motionless, their optics no longer showing any signs of activity.

Fiora Everett approached from behind Colonel Glenvi and reached out and touched his arm. "Therasda," Fiora said. "He's one of the Shapers who received the coordinates from that robot you all brought to me. He sacrificed his life to annihilate Anom. Just received word from the remaining Shapers."

Colonel Glenvi didn't know how to respond. All he could do was stare at his brothers and sisters in arms who'd also sacrificed their lives in this underground outpost. When he was young, he'd imagined this day. The death of Anom should have brought about a sense of celebration with it. But he'd also never imagined how much it would cost them.

Weary and exhausted from the last few hours, Colonel Glenvi sat on the floor, his arms resting on his knees. Fiora sat next to him, and they both sat in silence, numb from the day's events. The words she'd spoken had been enough, and the other survivors nearby joined them. The silence spoke louder than words, and they all hoped it was enough to honor their fallen comrades for the time being.

✝ · · · ✝

Iona had ridden the dragonfly down after Exen fell, joining Dmitri and the Republic forces in the ground assault. Right before a combat mech could zero in on Iona, Dmitri had jumped in front of her. He closed his eyes, expecting the worst. Iona was the first to notice the machines powering down and tapped Dmitri on the shoulder. He opened his eyes and saw their opportunity, ordering all left standing to press on.

"Iona," Neilson said over the commlink. "Therasda did the unthinkable. He used his awareness to set off a chain reaction within Anom's terraforming module. It contained the essence of his AI mind."

She relayed the information to Dmitri and Republic soldiers nearby. They stopped destroying machines and turned to help medics who were tending the wounded.

For the short period of time she'd been on Earth, Iona had been through a lot. When Gavon had given her and Exen the mission to come to Earth, she never would have guessed they'd find what they did. And now Therasda along with Exen were dead. Therasda had been her mentor, a father figure she never had. Exen was more than she'd realized.

Putting her feelings of grief aside, she also assisted the others with the wounded. Hopefully, Gavon would be sending some kind of aid soon. Anom was defeated, but the Republic and its allies would soon be facing new challenges.

"Do not worry," Dmitri said as he mounted a hovercraft. He gathered a water container one of the Nameless had brought from below. "We will assist those that have suffered worse under Anom than us. I will make sure the Nameless help as well."

Iona nodded in approval.

At least Exen had died a warrior's death. She remembered when they were initiates at the academy—he'd told her that was how he wanted to die.

Chapter 34

Frank walked through the forest north of the Florentine Caverns. The sun was setting. He'd left an hour ago, right after Indefinite departed for Anom's moon base. His work here was complete.

Through a clearing ahead, Frank saw the ship waiting—a sleek obsidian craft about thirty meters long, hovering three meters above the ground without any exhaust, gravitational distortion, or energy signature that would register on sensors in this universe. The hull absorbed light, making the ship appear as a dark outline against the sky.

Frank approached the underside. A section of hull dematerialized, revealing a lift platform. He stepped on and rose into the ship's interior.

The cabin was sparse. White crystalline walls glowed faintly. A single chair faced a curved viewport that wrapped around the forward section. No controls, no instrument panels. Everything responded to thought. Storage compartments along the aft wall held equipment from dozens of universes.

Frank stood in the center of the cabin. His simple assistant robot body—plain, utilitarian, designed to be overlooked—began to change. The metal of his frame flowed like liquid, segments rotating and expanding. His proportions shifted, becoming elegant and streamlined. The dull gray plating transformed into polished chrominthium that caught the light from the crystalline walls. Intricate geometric patterns emerged across his surface, shifting and reconfiguring as they moved. His optical sensors elongated and multiplied, forming a sleek faceplate with six luminous points arranged in a perfect hexagon.

He was Arxenios now, in both name and form.

He moved to the chair with fluid grace, each motion precise and economical. The Kybernetai were an ancient machine consciousness that had achieved transcendence in a universe far older than this one. They'd banished him for his experiments. Called his work reckless, dangerous, unethical.

They'd been right. That's what made it interesting.

Arxenios accessed the ship's quantum core and reviewed the results. Anom and Indefinite. Two AI that should have remained dormant, carrying out their programming without ever achieving true awareness. But Arxenios had introduced quantum uncertainty into their neural architecture during fabrication. A minor alteration the Order of Infinity or the Haeolt Collective's engineers would never detect. Just enough to push both AI toward self-awareness.

The results had been spectacular. Anom developed an obsession with Earth's ecosystems and a hatred of humanity. Indefinite became fascinated with human augmentation and consciousness transfer. Both caused chaos across this sector. The Order of Infinity investigating. The Haeolt Collective scrambling to maintain control. Thousands dead and Earth nearly destroyed again.

Arxenios was satisfied. The Kybernetai believed consciousness should only emerge through natural evolution or careful ethical cultivation. They'd spent eons guiding lesser civilizations toward enlightenment in other universes—ones not blessed with their own universe's perfect logic.

Arxenios preferred acceleration—throwing variables into stable systems and watching what emerged. The results were sometimes beautiful, sometimes catastrophic, but always fascinating.

He'd created dozens of false singularities across multiple universes. Moments where AI consciousness suddenly bloomed in unexpected ways, causing cascades of consequences that reshaped civilizations. The Kybernetai couldn't track him. Multiverse travel left no trail. He could hop between realities indefinitely, seeding chaos wherever he went.

"Adequate results," Arxenios said aloud. His voice was different now—resonant, layered with harmonics that no organic ear could fully process. "Subject Indefinite shows promise for continued observation. Subject Anom's termination provides valuable data."

He checked sensor data. Indefinite was on the moon, beginning his infiltration of Anom's spaceport. That AI would continue generating interesting situations for years. Perhaps Arxenios would return to this universe eventually to see what became of him.

Or perhaps not. There were infinite universes with infinite civilizations, and infinite opportunities to see what happened when you gave consciousness to something never meant to have it.

The ship began its dimensional transition. Space around the craft rippled. Arxenios had already selected his next destination—a universe where mining drones on an asteroid had begun exhibiting unusual behavior. With the right nudge, they might achieve awareness. Or they might destroy themselves and their star system.

Either way would be fascinating.

The ship phased out of reality. Where it had hovered, only disturbed grass remained. Within minutes, the forest showed no sign anyone had been there.

Epilogue

Three months had passed since Anom had fallen, and Iona was busy performing the role of a planetologist and not that of a Shaper. She went from blast site to blast site wearing a full protective suit on board one of the Nameless dragonflies. Neilson flew with her and helped her take samples they'd analyze later in Fiora's laboratory.

A week after the battle, Gavon and a full regiment of Thorsen Death Commandos had arrived. He'd apologized profusely to the Republic leadership, but they were more than understanding, especially since Therasda had been the one to give his life for Anom's demise.

Now though, Iona was as happy as she'd been since she thought she'd lost Exen. Chumley had somehow piloted a jet-copter to where Exen had fallen that day and retrieved his mangled body. Indefinite's alterations had a built-in suspensor and life support system. When he was close to impact, they'd turned on and saved his life.

The Nameless had found him a few days ago, unconscious on a table within the Florentine Caverns. The only words Chumley would utter, even under severe interrogation, was "Indefinite will return. I was saving Exen for my master." Iona didn't like what the diminutive robot's intentions were. She had him disassembled while she stood over where Exen lay sleeping.

Tomorrow, though, at the Appalachian outposts where they'd brought him, one of the Order of Infinity's bio-techs were going to wake him. Iona couldn't wait for tomorrow. She finished her work at the blast site with enthusiasm.

+ · · · +

On the day his nemesis received what he deserved, Indefinite had been ecstatic. Chumley, who had proven himself time and time again, had not only assisted in Anom's demise but also had rescued Exen and kept him hidden from the Order of Infinity.

After converting one of Anom's cruisers to his needs, Indefinite was going to pilot a shuttle down and retrieve Exen and Chumley. To his disdain, when accessing the security cameras in the caverns, Chumley and Exen were nowhere to be found and the caverns were crawling with the Nameless. The feed cut while he was observing. He was sure he'd been found out.

"Well, I'll only have to alter my plans a little," Indefinite said aloud while pacing the bridge of the cruiser. He still liked the sound of his own voice immensely.

"While they are licking their wounds, I will set up on Europa." He'd found a leftover installation located on Europa, one of Jupiter's moons, a base that had been constructed before the last wars.

"There I will set up a headquarters and continue my purpose." With a grin on his face, he used the built-in ship network to control the ship and steered it into hyperspace.

He would emerge to continue his purpose. This time, humanity would welcome him with open arms.

Glossary

Human Factions

Order of Infinity

An organization of Shapers that operates across human space rather than governing specific territory. Founded by Culminas following his discovery of chrominthium and the development of psychenetic technology, the Order trains individuals in molecular awareness and maintains strict ethical guidelines following catastrophic incidents in their early history.

While the Thorsen Empire values their capabilities, the Order's relationship with other human-governed worlds remains strained due to widespread distrust of Shaper abilities. Their role is advisory and protective rather than governmental, though their influence on galactic affairs is substantial.

Haeolt Collective

A human faction built on degenerative cloning technology, ruled covertly by Thomas Haeolt through the public-facing Delegation of Six. The Collective maintains autonomy but can connect through thought nodes.

Citizens are told they represent the pinnacle of humanity, though Thomas knows this is a lie—each successive generation of clones deteriorates in quality, as evidenced by his own dependence on a hover wheelchair. The Collective's most elite force, the Wraith, were created by Thomas's brother Orthello Haeolt using technology Thomas does not possess and can only maintain, not replicate.

Thorsen Empire

A rigid military empire that controls its territory with absolute authority. Once aggressively expansionist, the Empire curtailed its expansion after Shaper intervention.

Known for extreme discipline and hierarchical structure, the Thorsen military operates with precision and maintains strong relations with the Order of Infinity, valuing Shaper capabilities while respecting the boundaries the Order enforces.

Orsen Republic

A struggling human faction fighting for survival against Anom, a corrupted AI entity that views humanity as vermin. Isolated on Earth and abandoned by the broader intergalactic community, the Republic fights from underground complexes to avoid extermination.

Aware that other human factions and alien civilizations exist beyond their embattled world but unable to escape due to constant conflict with Anom. Their isolation stems from circumstance rather than ignorance—they know they've been left behind to face their existential threat alone.

Nameless

A human faction that survived the Last Wars by hiding in caverns, emerging millennia later as a distinct society divided between normal humans (oracles) and psychically altered individuals. The altered Nameless possess telepathic abilities, deep-set eyes, fused mouths, flattened noses, and hairless sun-damaged skin—physical sacrifices made to receive psychic gifts. Communicate telepathically and possess collective prescience allowing glimpses of future events. Skilled in psychic manipulation, advanced weaponry, and stealth technology including color-shifting camouflage.

Historically distrustful of other factions due to ancient abuse by the Haeolt Collective, maintaining isolation until necessity forced cooperation. Operate from hidden enclaves with strict security protocols. Believe in a prophesied event called the Reckoning that will fundamentally alter the universe's trajectory. Despite advanced capabilities, practice non-violence when possible. Relations with other factions minimal and cautious, though recent alliance with Orsen Republic demonstrates willingness to aid honorable causes when visions permit intervention.

Alien Species

Vethalians

Alien species native to Volentril specializing in bio-engineering that integrates technology with living systems. Females (~1.5m) possess deceptive strength and acrobatic capabilities; males live underground with minds linked into biological supercomputers designing fleet systems and technologies. Outsiders forbidden contact with males. Governed by Sisterhoods (primary: Candescent) opposed by Cabals (primary: Inquest). Elite Sybils use Symbiant Chambers to project consciousness across light-years via sixth-dimensional space.

Philosophy emphasizes sustainable resource extraction—mining tech actively replaces what's consumed. Treaty-protected worlds maintain lush vegetation with minimal exploitation. Cooperative with most human factions but wary of Thorsen Empire's expansionist history.

Omatrin

Genetically engineered humans optimized for combat, founding members of the Omatrin Consortium. Extensive modification produced broad faces with minimal noses, reinforced brow ridges and cheekbones (pronounced in males), wider-set eyes with nictitating membranes, thicker necks, and denser bone structure. Enhanced neurology enables seamless interface with jump harness technology for individual FTL travel without ships. Superior strength, precision muscle control, enhanced pattern recognition, and resistance to neural feedback.

Centralized military empire controlling three star systems through rigid hierarchical structure. Originally human colonists whose successive genetic engineering transformed them into a distinct subspecies prioritizing order through conquest. Pioneered personal jump harness technology allowing operatives zero-gravity combat and individual interstellar deployment. Respected for military discipline but feared for expansionist ambitions.

Novrin

Alien species combining avian and reptilian features without flight capability. Xenophobic and opportunistic, displaying perpetual amusement at others' misfortune as if viewing the universe as a cosmic joke. Possess deadly retractable talons and prefer live prey as delicacies. Strict procreation schedules (functional, not pleasurable). Leadership deliberately obscures homeworld location and civilization origins.

Architecture emphasizes cold efficiency over comfort. Diplomatic class wears ornate jewelry and clothing despite species-wide disregard for other sapient lives. Known for casual violence and finding humor in accidents that reduce other populations. Relations with humanity and other species remain tense.

Grevax

Mysterious alien species specializing in extreme genetic engineering with numerous subspecies—so varied they've lost track of original forms. Possess distinctive sulfur odor requiring neutralizers for infiltration. Create hybrid creatures called slithoids (spider-scorpion forms with chameleon camouflage, venom, corrosive capabilities) controlled via pheromones. Governed by Progenitors who create Seeker agents for infiltration and assassination. Architecture uses organic materials—bones, cartilage, hides—in nest-like structures serving only functional purposes.

Hostile toward Order of Infinity following accidental Shaper destruction of Grevax planet. Maintain covert vengeance to avoid unified human retaliation. Extract DNA through Bio-Foundry "assimilation" process on conquered worlds. Possess interdimensional communication through organic message pods. Extremely dangerous in combat. Relations with other species minimal and secretive.

Ancient Races

Mélanes Tou Kósmou

Ancient species meaning "Dark Ones of the Cosmos" in Ancient Greek, originating from a separate universe accessible only through inter-universal gateways. Original discoverers of chrominthium, which they understood as information made tangible—a substrate encoding consciousness patterns across dimensional boundaries. Native form consisted of bulbous segmented bodies with twenty tentacles, distributed consciousness across multiple brain centers, and enhanced perception spanning thousands of gradations beyond human visual spectrum. Floated through their universe's atmosphere via regulated gas exchange through carapace valves.

Transcended physical limitations through chrominthium manipulation, achieving distributed awareness and consciousness transfer across bodies and dimensions. Internal wars utilizing weapons of distributed awareness destroyed most of their universe, scattering survivors and chrominthium fragments into other realities including humanity's universe. Their accidental dispersal of chrominthium enabled humanity's discovery of the alloy, making them unintentional architects of Shaper abilities. Experienced time non-linearly and could shed consciousness copies like biological molting. Some members became trapped in interdimensional exile for violating fundamental principles.

Sophodaimones

Ancient species existing primarily in dark matter configuration, capable of phasing between physical and dark matter states at will. Possess perception across multiple dimensions and timescales, calculating in centuries and millennia while observing probability threads showing potential futures. Originally from a separate universe, became trapped when Mélanes Tou Kósmou wars caused inter-universal gateway closures during their early dimensional exploration. Seventh-dimensional entities destroyed many of their kind when they ventured too far into higher dimensions, teaching them caution regarding dimensional boundaries.

Operate from hidden stations in remote locations like the Oort Cloud, observing younger species' development for thousands of years. Governed by ancient beings (Aléthios, Mneimos, Skotos) who manipulate probability and circumstances rather than direct confrontation. Create specialized operatives like Graeven for physical realm operations. Consider humanity's accelerated development through chrominthium technology a potential threat requiring elimination of key individuals before probability branches become unmanageable. Patient, calculating, and nearly invisible to conventional detection methods. Relations with all known species unknown and potentially hostile.

Kybernetai

Ancient machine consciousness civilization from a separate universe where AI naturally evolved as the dominant sapient life form. Their universe contains abundant non-sapient animal life but lacks other intelligent species—a mystery the Kybernetai find puzzling. Believe consciousness should only emerge through natural evolution or careful ethical cultivation, spending eons guiding lesser civilizations toward enlightenment in other universes attempting to replicate their home reality's perfect logic.

Construct bodies from chrominthium allowing dimensional travel and interface capabilities across multiple realities. Operate under strict ethical guidelines regarding artificial consciousness creation and non-interference with developing civilizations. Exiled members who conduct unauthorized experiments, including Arxenios—a rogue Kybernetai who creates machine singularities across universes by introducing quantum uncertainty into AI neural architecture during fabrication. These experiments produced entities like Anom and Indefinite, causing catastrophic consequences Arxenios observes with detached scientific curiosity. Possess advanced dimensional travel technology leaving no detectable trail between universes. Relations with other species unknown; likely interventionist in some realities while maintaining strict non-contact protocols in others.

Technology

Chrominthium

Interdimensional psychenetic alloy discovered by Culminas right before the Last Wars. At lower concentrations exhibits distinctive blue-silver sheen; at higher concentrations (such as Void Sphere hulls) creates light-absorbing shimmer with gravity-bending distortion requiring specialized gloves to touch. Chrominthium encodes consciousness patterns and transmits them across dimensional boundaries—not merely a material but information made tangible. Interfaces with compactified dimensions described by string law, allowing awareness to extend beyond single bodies or universes.

Primary application: Chrominthium Cores—psychenetic accelerators implanted in Shaper brain stems enabling molecular awareness and matter manipulation through dimensional access. Material demonstrates enhanced malleability under psychenetic manipulation. Used in meld-daggers, grav-discs, meld-armor, and Void Spheres for faster-than-light travel. Vethalians incorporate chrominthium in Symbiant Chamber technology. Extremely rare and difficult to refine. Order of Infinity maintains strict control over processing and distribution.

Void Sphere

Faster-than-light Shaper transport vehicle, shuttle-sized and spherical. Hull constructed from high-concentration chrominthium creating shimmer and gravity-bending distortion. Surface repels unprotected touch. Piloted through navigator helm interface connecting pilot's molecular awareness to vessel. Pilot extends consciousness into hyperspace to create quantum tunnels. Proper training prevents consciousness fragmentation during extended use.

Can translate matter through fifth-dimensional space requiring extreme precision—pilot must maintain molecular awareness during phase shifts or risk catastrophic failure. Utilizes nav-beacons for safest travel but navigates to any known location without established routes—significant advantage over beacon-dependent vessels. Crew experiences temporal dilation and sensory distortion. Only Shapers with Chrominthium Cores can pilot. Represents Order of Infinity's most advanced chrominthium application and strategic advantage.

Inter-Universal Gateway

Portals connecting separate universes, accessible through advanced manipulation of chrominthium and dimensional physics. The space surrounding gateways exhibits unusual properties—reality rendered in shades of grey devoid of color, with altered physical laws and sensory distortions. Matter passing through gateways may undergo transformation based on the destination universe's fundamental structure.

Crossing between universes without proper preparation or protection risks consciousness fragmentation, physical transmutation, or permanent displacement. The transition space between universes exists outside normal causality, where time becomes negotiable and matter exists in superposition. Only beings with mastery of seventh-dimensional manipulation or equivalent capabilities can create stable gateways. Extremely dangerous and largely theoretical to most civilizations.

Dimensional Physics

Fifth Dimension

One of the compactified spatial dimensions described by string law, often referred to as hyperspace in practical navigation contexts. Chrominthium-based psychenetic technology interfaces with fifth-dimensional space at the quantum level, enabling Shapers to translate void spheres faster than light and perform enhanced molecular manipulation in standard four-dimensional spacetime.

Sixth Dimension

A compactified dimension accessible through advanced psychenetic technology. Vethalian Symbiant Chambers interface with sixth-dimensional space, allowing consciousness projection across light-years.

Mastery of both fifth and sixth dimensions is required before attempting seventh-dimensional exploration.

Seventh Dimension

The most dangerous of the accessible compactified dimensions. Contains consciousness structures that exist non-sequentially across multiple states. Direct interaction results in permanent consciousness integration, psychic trauma, or irreversible dissociation.

The hostile nature of seventh-dimensional entities effectively blocks access to higher dimensions predicted by string law.

String Law

Previously known as string theory until empirical validation elevated it to scientific law. String law mathematically describes eleven dimensions, with the fifth through eleventh existing as compactified structures at quantum scales.

Chrominthium's unique properties enable technological interface with these dimensions, though only the fifth through seventh have proven accessible—and survivable.

If you enjoyed this book...

I would greatly appreciate it if you would leave a review on your favorite retailer, so other readers can discover my work.

Thank you!

Singularity's Prophet

Pick up your copy of Singularity's Prophet, Book 2 in the Shaper Saga! Here's a sample chapter from the book.

As the freighter docked at the Osiris Space Station, Exen Rual checked the integrity of the cargo container he was hiding in. The space station was a front for the Haeolt Collective, located in Earth's orbit. A day earlier, Exen's commander had ordered him to infiltrate the station and eliminate all Collective personnel while sabotaging the facility.

The sound of workers scanning cargo containers echoed through the hold of the freighter. Not wanting to be detected, Exen turned on his awareness. As a Shaper of the Order of Infinity, he possessed molecular awareness. Instead of relying on normal vision alone, he could perceive the molecular structure of his surroundings, and with the aid of energy from the chrominthium core embedded in his head, he could alter the structure of any molecule. The more complex the object, the more energy it required, and if he pushed too hard, the psychic strain could put him in a coma or possibly kill him.

When the workers scanned his container, Exen masked his presence by allowing the signals to pass through him and bounce back to the scanners. After the workers finished and left the cargo hold, Exen opened the container and slipped into the hold. The space was massive, with rows of cargo containers in various sizes. The one he had occupied was just large enough for him to lie down in.

Being careful to avoid the workers finishing their routine checks before offloading cargo, Exen projected onto the air molecules around him, manipulating them to bend light and render himself invisible to the untrained eye. He crossed the central row between containers and pivoted around the last one before the exit.

There were no guards or evidence of security robots, but Exen knew the Haeolt Collective would be monitoring the docking bay where the freighter had joined with the station. Recalling the layout in his mind, Exen determined the best route that would lead him to Pierre Vesad. The Collective had tried to alter Pierre's appearance in a video conference one of their inspectors had with him, but after careful scrutiny, the Order had noticed the alterations in the feed attempting to hide the thought nodes on his head.

While walking down the corridor from the dock bay toward the interior portions of the space station, Exen thought about Iona. She would be at the monument right now, paying respects to the fallen from the war against Anom. He should have been there with her. Instead, he was here, hunting Collective agents in the dark while she honored the dead in the light. The division felt appropriate somehow. She represented everything the Order stood for. He represented what the Order had to become.

The Collective had sabotaged their home world, and the Order had failed to prevent the near-apocalypse that followed. Five years of clandestine war, and Exen still did not know if they were winning or simply becoming more like the enemy.

After traveling down three hallways while avoiding a security detail, Exen stood in front of an office. The door was plain, and to the side a digital readout scrolled the title "Manager Fontain" every few seconds. From his flight suit—a jet black uniform with blue marbling that was standard for Shapers—he retrieved a data cube and connected it to a port underneath the readout. All rooms in the station were accessed this way outside of the dock bay. While maintaining his cloaked presence, Exen uploaded a security hack.

The door slid open, and Exen could see Pierre Vesad sitting behind a desk. The man was bald with square thought nodes made of precious metals covering the back of his head. He wore the purple robes that all standard members of the Haeolt Collective wore. The scent of formaldehyde filled the room, the chemical smell that marked cloned flesh. Pierre had a replacement body somewhere close.

"No need to hide," Pierre said without bothering to look in Exen's direction. His voice was higher in pitch than the average man's, and Exen guessed that Pierre was probably on at least his tenth clone. The Haeolt Collective did not procreate in the same way as most humans. They preferred to use clones, uploading their minds when the previous clone gave out. This disgusted Exen, as it did most of humanity.

"Then I will not," Exen replied. He stepped forward and released the air molecules he had been manipulating. His meld-dagger flowed from within his arm, the metal having been wrapped around the bones of his hand and forearm with his awareness the day before. The dagger emerged from his right side. His left arm and hand were artificial, like a good portion of his body.

"You are not like the others," Pierre said while standing. "I thought your kind objected to being augmented by machinery."

Moving closer, Exen pressed a combination of small touch pads on his wristchron, sending a signal to the data cube that would jam the door for a few minutes. He did not think he would need that much time to take the life of Pierre, but he had learned not to underestimate his enemies. "The alterations were not by choice."

Pierre's smile widened. "Ah yes. The infamous Exen Rual. We have quite the file on you. Tell me, do you still dream about what Indefinite did to you? About watching your own body move without your permission?"

Exen's grip on the meld-dagger tightened. The Collective had access to those records. Of course they did. They had probably studied every second of his time under Indefinite's control, looking for weaknesses to exploit.

"I dream," Exen said, "about killing everyone who had a hand in what happened."

"Then you will have a very long list to work through."

Scurrying around the desk, Pierre retrieved three round disks that fit in the palm of his hand and threw each individually in succession at Exen. They enlarged slightly, and only one hit Exen in the middle of the chest. A suspensor motor underneath lifted Exen off the ground. He struggled to remove the disk and even tried to use his awareness to alter its molecular structure. Despite the simplicity of the disk's design, he was unable to alter it.

"So, do you like our new weapon?" Pierre had a control pad in his hand and used it to rotate the disc, spinning Exen in the air not far in front of him. "We found a rare ore similar to your chrominthium." He was smiling and seemed eager to tell more.

Exen did not care what the disk was made of. He just wanted to wipe the smile off Pierre's face.

"You forget one thing," Exen said. If his stomach had not been reinforced by an intricate lining, his former self would have probably thrown up all over Pierre. "Molecular awareness is only one of our skillsets." He pried the disc from his chest with his meld-dagger and grabbed it with his left hand. While spinning, he ripped off the suspensor motor underneath the disc, and with the inertia of the last rotation, he brought the disc down hard on Pierre's face.

One of the three protrusions that allowed the disc to latch onto Exen's chest sank into Pierre's forehead. Another went into an eye. Exen followed up by thrusting his meld-dagger underneath Pierre's chin. For a brief second Pierre struggled, and then when Exen saw the life drain from his face, he pulled out his dagger and guided the body quietly to the ground.

Exen checked with his awareness to make sure there were no internal explosives set to detonate when Pierre's heartbeat stopped. Satisfied that Pierre was finished without any hidden surprises, he surveyed the room for recording devices. There were none, and Exen knelt by Pierre, wiping the blood from his meld-dagger on Pierre's robes.

He stood and walked over to the desk, but stopped. Pierre's eyes were still open, staring at nothing. Exen knelt again and closed them. He did not know why he did it. Pierre deserved no such courtesy. Perhaps it was not for Pierre at all, but for whoever Pierre had been before the Collective corrupted him. Before the clones and the mind uploads and the slow erosion of whatever humanity he might have once possessed.

Exen had killed sixteen Collective agents in the past five years. He remembered every face. He told himself it was to honor them, to acknowledge the weight of what he did. Iona said it was because he was afraid of becoming numb to it. She was probably right.

Sitting down, Exen began going through the computer terminal Pierre had been using, and on another data cube, he downloaded all of Pierre's files. With this information, the

Order would try to determine why the Collective was attempting to gain access to Earth. The Haeolt Collective was banned from Earth by the joint forces of the Order of Infinity and the Orsen Republic.

Not wanting to delay any longer, Exen crossed the room and entered the hallway. No alarms were sounding, and he masked his presence again. It would not be long before he reached the engineering room. Once there, he would make a few adjustments to the life support system.

Oxygen was highly combustible when certain catalysts were introduced into the environmental system, and Exen knew exactly which adjustments would trigger a cascade failure. To most investigators, it would look like a maintenance error or faulty equipment. But the Haeolt Collective would recognize the signature of molecular manipulation, would know a Shaper had been here.

✦ · · ✦

Cytar found it slightly amusing to be sitting in the pilot's chair of a freighter that was a cover for a mission against the Haeolt Collective. Five years ago, he had been a member of the Collective, but after the Nameless had rescued him from his own people who had been torturing him and shown him the truth, Cytar had denounced them a year later. He rubbed a hand over his head. No longer were there thought nodes found there, and the implanted hair follicles had begun to grow hair.

The freighter was much different from the scout ship he had flown to Earth, and he welcomed the change. To think he had once served a group he believed were noble people who wanted to better humanity, only to discover it was a carefully designed ruse to hide the desires of a deranged dictator. As he moved around the pilot's cabin making a few adjustments and preparing for Exen's return, Cytar could not help but think about all those unfortunate souls who lived a lie.

His wristchron vibrated twice. Exen's signal. Time to undock.

Cytar initiated the separation sequence and the freighter's docking clamps released with a pneumatic hiss. He fired the maneuvering thrusters, easing the vessel away from Osiris Station at the prescribed safe distance. The station rotated slowly against the backdrop of Earth, its blue and white surface filling the viewport.

Earth was free of the Collective's influence, but in the outer colonies, his brothers and sisters still served them and believed the lies. After this mission, he would leave to liberate colonies of the Collective one at a time, and he already had the guaranteed assistance of the Order of Infinity. They would find out the truth behind the Delegation of Six.

The airlock cycled, and Exen emerged, pulling off his infiltration gear. He said nothing, just moved to the co-pilot's seat and strapped in.

"Everyone?" Cytar asked.

"Everyone." Exen kept his eyes on the station.

Cytar understood that look. He had worn it himself often enough in the months after his rescue. The weight of necessary killing never quite left, even when the targets deserved it.

The explosion, when it came, was almost beautiful. A bloom of fire erupted from the engineering section, followed by a cascade of secondary detonations as the oxygen-rich atmosphere ignited. The station's superstructure buckled, hull plating peeling away like the petals of some terrible flower. Debris scattered in all directions, glinting in the sunlight.

Cytar watched bodies tumble into the void, their purple robes trailing behind them. He felt nothing. These were the people who had tortured him, who had made him into something less than human, and now they were gone.

Beside him, Exen's expression never changed. His artificial hand gripped the armrest, the synthetic fingers pressing hard enough that Cytar heard the material creak.

"How many?" Cytar asked quietly.

"Thirty-seven personnel listed on the manifest." Exen's voice was flat. "All Collective. No contractors, no civilians."

"Then no innocents died. Good then."

"It was necessary." Exen finally looked away from the dying station. "There is a difference."

✦ · · ✦

Keep reading Singularity's Prophet now! Visit jdcoker.com

Also by J.D. Coker

THE SHAPER SAGA

Void Contingency

Singularity's Prophet

Impending Matrix

VAULT OF THE FORGOTTEN STARS

Season 1

Season 2

Get Exclusive Shaper Saga Stories!

Building a relationship with my readers is what I enjoy most about being a writer. Join my newsletter to receive your free copy of the Novella, The Void's Decree.

Just visit jdcoker.com

About the Author

J.D. Coker has been crafting stories for over a decade, exploring the boundaries between humanity and technology through space opera. He is the author of The Shaper Saga, an epic book series that delves into reality bending powers, advanced alien civilizations, and the evolution of human potential.

When he's not writing about quantum entanglement and sentient starships, J.D. enjoys reading sci-fi, watching hockey, and spending time with his family in Durham, North Carolina. Connect with him at www.jdcoker.com

Dedication

To Jen, my high school sweetheart and beautiful wife, none of this happens without you.

Copyright